Usborne
One Hundred Illustrated Stories

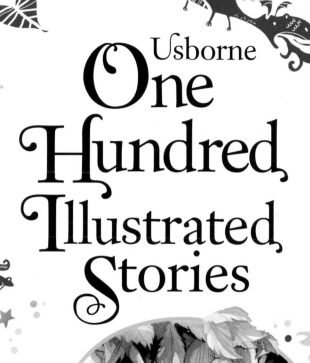

Contents

Stories retold by
Sarah Courtauld, Susanna Davidson,
Katie Daynes, Rosie Dickins, Russell Punter,
Mary Sebag-Montefiore and Lesley Sims

Illustrations by
Lorena Alvarez, Poly Bernatene, Gabo León Bernstein,
Fred Blunt, Petra Brown, Simona Bursi, Stephen Cartwright,
Francesca di Chiara, Lee Cosgrove, Jana Costa, Ciaran Duffy,
Jacqueline East, Frank Endersby, Merel Eyckerman, Fabiano Fiorin,
Laure Fournier, Mike and Carl Gordon, Teri Gower,
Desideria Guicciardini, Daniel Howarth, Ann Kronheimer,
Qin Leng, Raffaella Ligi, Ali Lodge, Katie Lovell, Anna Luraschi,
Ben Mantle, Alan Marks, Rocío Martínez, Alida Massari,
Jan McCafferty, Paddy Mounter, Kelly Murphy, Eva Muszynski,
John Nez, Eugenia Nobati, Germano Ovani, Georgien Overwater,
Graham Philpot, Daniel Postgate, Jenny Press, Nathalie Ragondet,
Sara Rojo, Simona Sanfilippo, Kate Sheppard, Elisa Squillace,
Victor Tavares, Elena Temporin, Barbara Vagnozzi,
Emilie Vanvolsem and Matt Ward

Foreword

The stories you are about to read come from all over the world. Some are thousands of years old, some were written only a few hundred years ago, but they all have one thing in common: they capture the imagination and linger long after these pages are closed.

You may know some of the stories already, others may be new to you. One thing that might surprise you is how different cultures, separated by thousands of miles and hundreds of years, came up with such similar tales. It seems that everyone loves stories of bravery and trickery, rewards and revenge, magic and mischief.

Would you like to explore far-off lands on a flying carpet, battle witches and giants, meet princes and princesses and discover deep secrets?

Then read on...

Once upon
a time...

The Emperor's New Clothes

There was once an Emperor who was so fond of clothes, he hardly thought about anything else. He ignored important business and avoided his advisors. He preferred to spend his days in front of a mirror, trying on fancy, frilly shirts and preposterous pantaloons.

One day, two strangers came to see him. "We make the finest clothes in the world," they said smoothly. "In fact, they are so incredible, they can only be seen by clever people."

"Really?" said the Emperor.

"Oh yes," said the men. "They're completely invisible to anyone stupid – or anyone who can't do their job properly."

The Emperor rubbed his chin. "They sound astonishing," he chuckled. "Make me a new outfit at once! It'll be just the thing for my next procession. I want something so amazing, people will talk about it for years!"

"It won't be cheap," warned the men.

"I don't care!" the Emperor declared. And he gave the men a sackful of money.

Several days later, with a great fanfare, the men unveiled the new clothes...

The Emperor gulped. He stared. He couldn't see a thing! "I must be a terrible emperor," he thought. But out loud, he said, "Wonderful!"

Nervously, he tried to put on the invisible outfit. Carefully, the men buttoned invisible buttons and tied invisible ribbons into invisible bows.

"How do I look?" asked the Emperor.

His advisors glanced at each other. They couldn't see anything either, but they didn't dare to say so. "Magnificent!" they cried.

So the Emperor set out proudly on the procession. A huge crowd had gathered to see his new clothes. Everyone had heard only clever people could see them. "Amazing," they told each other... until a small voice piped up.

"Ooh," said a little boy. "The Emperor's got no clothes on!"

The people around him took another look. "He's right you know," they began to laugh. "The Emperor's got no clothes!"

The Emperor glanced down – and blushed from head to toe. "I've been tricked!" he realized. But there was a procession to finish. So he held his head high and strode on.

"At least this is an outfit they'll always remember," he sighed.

The Town Mouse and the Country Mouse

Johnny Town Mouse put his paws in his pockets and whistled to the wind as he sauntered down the country lane. At last, he came to a little door in the hedge, half-covered with ivy, and knocked.

"Surprise!" he called, as Pipin, his country cousin, unlatched the door. "I've come to stay!"

"Then it's time for a feast," cried Pipin. He gathered up nuts and berries, cups of dew, and pieces of honeycomb laid out on a rush grass plate.

Johnny Town Mouse put his nose in
the air. "Oh dear!" he sneered. He
flicked away a berry with his paw.
"This isn't *my* idea of a feast.
And where am I to sleep?"
He pointed at Pipin's mossy
mattress. "Not there!"

"That *is* where I sleep..." Pipin began.

"No, no. This won't do," Johnny Town
Mouse declared. "I think I've had enough of
your country life. Let's go to town and live
like kings."

The mice ran to the station and scampered
on board a train. It pulled away with a jolt and
a blast, rattling over the tracks.

Pipin gazed out of the window. He watched
as tall trees turned to houses. He sniffed
smoke and sausages on the air.

"We're here! We're here!" cried Johnny
Town Mouse.

They ran across the station, dodging between stamping feet.

"So many people…" thought Pipin, his heart pounding with fear.

They ran down dirty pavements, past belching buses and vrooming cars, until they came to a towering town house.

"Impressed?" asked Johnny Town Mouse, casually pointing his paw.

"Very," nodded Pipin.

"Now," said Johnny, "I'll show you a feast."

He led Pipin to the dining room, and a table groaning with food. Pipin's eyes grew rounder and rounder. And then they began to eat… ice cream and pie, chocolate and cheese, huge slices of cake topped with raspberry cream.

Pipin clutched his tummy and shut his eyes. "How wonderful," he sighed, "to live like this always."

"You think?" purred a voice in his ear.

"Oh no!" cried Johnny Town Mouse. "It's the cat!"

The mice ran this way and that. After them pounced the hungry cat.

"Quick!" called Johnny Town Mouse. "Into this hole."

"Oh my paws and whiskers," said Pipin, sinking to the floor. "*Please*, take me home."

Back to the station they ran, dancing in and out of rushing feet... and Pipin dashed onto the train. He looked out of the window and waved to his cousin. "Goodbye! Goodbye!"

Johnny Town Mouse ran beside the train. "Stay with me!" he called.

Pipin just shook his head.

The train chugged away, leaving the city behind. Finally, in the starry dark, Pipin reached his hedge. All was quiet. All was calm. He sniffed the cold, sweet air and smiled.

"Better nuts and berries in peace than cake and cream in fear," thought Pipin. "This is the life for me."

Beauty and the Beast

Once there was a merchant who had three daughters. The two eldest were petty and selfish, but the youngest was so lovely that she was called Beauty.

When Beauty was seventeen, the merchant had to go away on business. "I'll bring gifts for you all," he said. "What would you like?"

"I want pearls," demanded the eldest.

"Get me diamonds," ordered the second.

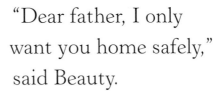

"Dear father, I only want you home safely," said Beauty.

"But you must have a present too," her father insisted.

"In that case, may I have a red rose?" Beauty asked.

Her father smiled. He didn't see her sisters sneering; he didn't know they were jealous of Beauty's sweetness.

Months later, as he journeyed home, the merchant lost his way. He'd bought pearls and diamonds for his elder daughters, but he hadn't found a red rose anywhere. Weary from wandering, he stumbled upon the entrance to a castle.

As he approached, he felt invisible hands leading him inside, where a delicious feast was set out. After he'd eaten, the hands took him to a luxurious bedroom. Never had he known such comfort.

The next morning, walking in the gardens after breakfast, he saw a rosebush blooming with glorious red roses.

"Beauty's present!" he thought. "I'm sure no one will mind if I pick just one," and he clasped the stem of the loveliest rose.

As he touched it, a voice roared, "After all I have offered you, how dare you steal one of my flowers?"

The merchant spun around and was overwhelmed with horror. Standing before him was a hideous beast with thick hairy limbs, cruel pointed horns and jagged fangs.

"I - I just wanted a present for my daughter," he stuttered.

"You may take her my rose," thundered the Beast, "if you promise to send to me whoever greets you first on your return."

Surely, reasoned the merchant silently, *that will be my dog.* "I promise," he said, thinking of his dog running to meet him...

...but it was Beauty who rushed into his arms before anyone else.

"Oh no," whispered the merchant.

"Why do you say that, Father? What a beautiful rose you've brought me!"

He told her everything, holding her tight. "I can't let you go to that monster."

"But I must. You promised," Beauty said.

Her sisters, secretly thrilled to think of Beauty banished to the Beast's castle, agreed.

Bravely, Beauty went.

When she arrived at the castle, she found music playing, a sumptuous feast laid out, and rooms prepared for her hung with dazzling silks. There was no sign of the Beast until the evening, when she sat down to supper and the doors to the dining room opened.

It was the Beast. Beauty gasped. He was even more terrifying than her father had described, but he asked politely, "May I eat with you?"

Shuddering at his repulsiveness, Beauty forced herself to answer, "Yes."

He was so interesting to talk to, her fear swiftly died away. Beauty relaxed, enjoying his company.

Weeks passed. The Beast was thoughtful, kind, gentle and full of funny stories, as they talked over meals, read to each other or walked in the gardens.

They spent every day together, until one day he asked,

"Will you marry me?"

"Ugh! He's too ugly," Beauty thought. "I couldn't," she replied, adding, as his eyes filled with tears, "I'm so sorry."

That very night, she had a nightmare of her father dying, as her sisters ignored him to try on new dresses. In the morning, she couldn't stop worrying. She was so sad that the Beast let her go home.

"But come back to me soon – please," he begged.

"I promise," swore Beauty.

Her father was overjoyed to see her. He wasn't dying, but he had missed her every day and had been sick with worry.

Her sisters claimed to be pleased, but they were furious to see her return.

"If Beauty doesn't leave," they whispered to each other, "the Beast will be angry that she's broken her promise and he'll punish her. Let's pretend we really missed her too."

The trick worked.

Beauty stayed... and stayed... Though she loved being at home, her thoughts kept going back to the Beast, remembering only his kindness and how he made her smile.

"I wish I could see him," she murmured, one evening, "just to know that he's well and happy."

In one swift moment, she felt herself swept through the air, back to his castle. As she stepped through the familiar garden, she saw the Beast lying on the ground, groaning pitifully, his eyes closed.

He looked almost dead.

"Beast!" she cried, running to kneel by his side. As she stroked his face, she no longer saw his ugliness. She knew, beyond doubt, that she loved him.

"You broke your promise..." he gasped. "You didn't come back."

"I'm here now," Beauty sobbed. "How can I save you? "

"Marry me," he breathed.

She kissed his brow. "With all my heart, dear Beast."

At these words, the Beast's hideous body vanished, and a handsome prince was standing before her.

"Oh Beauty, thank you! I was under an enchantment," he explained. "Many years ago, a wicked magician turned me into a beast. He declared that's how I would stay."

The prince smiled. "I had just one hope of escape..." he went on, "...if a beautiful girl were to kiss me and promise to marry me. I didn't think it would happen."

Within days, they were married, and they lived happily ever after. Beauty's sisters eventually found husbands of their own and stopped being jealous of her, and her father's old age was cheered by seeing the joy of his youngest daughter with her prince.

The Magic Carpet

Princess Nura didn't know what to do. Three princes wanted to marry her, and she didn't know whom to choose. So she decided to set a challenge. "I'll marry whoever brings me the rarest treasure!" she said.

The princes searched far and wide. Prince Ali found an ivory telescope, which showed whatever you wanted to see. Prince Ahmed bought a sweet-smelling apple, which could cure any illness. And Prince Hasan met a beautiful woman, who gave him a flying carpet.

He was speeding along on it when he
spotted Ali and Ahmed looking worried.
"What's the matter?" he called.

Ali waved an ivory telescope. "I saw Nura,"
he cried. "She's been taken ill!"

"My apple will cure her," Ahmed added, "if
we can reach her in time."

"No problem," replied Hasan. "Climb on!"

Minutes later, they were at the palace. Nura
was terribly pale. But as soon as she smelled
the apple, pink returned to her cheeks.

Nura couldn't decide which of the treasures
was best, so she set another challenge. "Who
can shoot the furthest?" she asked.

The princes picked up their bows. Ahmed's arrow went far, but Ali's went further. Then it was Hasan's turn. His arrow soared into the air – and vanished altogether.

"That's a forfeit," said Ali. "Who knows where it landed? So I win!" He knelt before the princess. "Will you be mine?"

"Yes," replied Nura, beaming.

Ahmed turned away – only to notice another girl smiling shyly at him. "She's even more lovely than Nura," he thought.

"Let me introduce my sister," said Nura.

It was love at first sight for the couple.

Ahmed laughed with delight. "It seems things have worked out for the best," he said.

Now Hasan was all alone with the carpet. To his surprise, he didn't feel at all sad. Instead, his thoughts turned to the woman who had given him the carpet.

"I wish I could see her again," he sighed.

Before he had even finished speaking, the carpet quivered and began to rise. He jumped on, and they flew over rooftops and trees, and golden desert sands, to land beside a familiar figure. Hasan's heart did a somersault.

"You're the one!" he exclaimed. "Are you a fairy?"

"Yes," she said. "Forgive me for magicking away your arrow, but I couldn't let you win. The princess really loved Ali."

"I'm glad," admitted Hasan. "Especially to see you again." He blushed and added, "I think I'd like to marry *you*."

The fairy smiled. "Nothing would make me happier," she said. "Now we can all live happily ever after – and that's the best magic of all."

The Goose That Laid The Golden Eggs

Emily and Daniel lived on a little farm, high up in the mountains. They were poor, but they were happy. They had a goat that gave them creamy milk, and hens and geese that gave them fresh eggs.

Every morning, Daniel got up to collect the eggs and take them down to the village to sell. But one morning, as he was plucking eggs out of the straw, he picked up one that was cool and heavy, and not at all like the others.

He rubbed his eyes, blinked, and stared at it, completely perplexed.

Soon the mysterious egg was lying, shining brightly, on the kitchen table, with Emily and Daniel gazing down at it.

"It looks like gold," Emily said slowly. "But it couldn't actually be gold... Could it?"

There was only one way to find out. Daniel took it to the village goldsmith, who peered at it, tapped it with a hammer, and handed it back to him with a grin.

"That," said the goldsmith, "is a solid gold egg. I'll give you one hundred gold coins for it."

In a daze, Daniel took the bag full of coins – more money than he had ever seen in his life – and walked through the village, buying a dress, shoes and hat for Emily.

He ran back to their farm, his arms full of presents. Emily was overjoyed.

She put on all her new clothes, and they danced around their yard, astounded at their good fortune.

The next morning, Daniel walked nervously into the hen house to collect the eggs. There, nestled in the straw, was another shining golden egg, next to a perfectly ordinary-looking white goose.

"It's incredible!" Daniel shouted, and he ran all the way to the village, to sell the egg to the goldsmith. The next day, the goose laid another shiny gold egg. And the day after that, sure enough, she laid another one.

Soon, Daniel and Emily were rich beyond their wildest dreams. They bought beautiful new clothes. They employed servants to do all the work on their farm and they moved to a much bigger house, with an enormous orchard.

At first, their new life seemed perfect. But after a while, they wondered if their house was big enough.

"We need more rooms," Emily sighed. "Fifteen just isn't enough. We need one for my dresses, one for our books, one for *my* musical instruments, one to sleep in, one for *your* musical instruments, and at least three for the servants..."

Daniel looked around him, and realized that the house, which had seemed so huge, was actually tiny.

"We'll have to move," he said, frowning. "What we really need is a massive house, with a large park around it – so the people next door can't stare in at us all the time."

Emily and Daniel thought about it and decided that they needed at least fifty rooms.

"That's settled," said Emily. "Let's move as soon as possible."

"We can't," Daniel said gloomily. "We simply don't have enough money."

Daniel and Emily walked into the hen house, and looked down at the little white goose.

"If the goose keeps laying one egg a day," said Daniel, "it will take us years to be able to pay for the mansion we need."

"Lots of the other geese lay two, three or four eggs a day," said Emily. "Why can't this goose lay more than one?"

The goose looked up at them. Annoyed, they glared back.

"There's no solution," Emily said, finally. "We'll just have to make do."

But at breakfast the next morning, Daniel jumped up from the table.

"Every day, the goose lays a golden egg," he began. "But where does the gold come from?"

Emily looked at Daniel, puzzled.

"Don't you see?" he said. "The goose must be full of gold."

"Of course!" said Emily.

"We just need to get it..."

They both rushed to the hen house. Emily took hold of the goose, while Daniel struck it on the head, and killed it.

"Inside this goose, we're going to find more gold than we've ever seen," Daniel murmured. But when he cut it open, his face fell. There was no gold inside.

Emily turned on him, with a face like thunder. "Daniel, what have you done?"

"Well, it wasn't me who insisted on a new house!" shouted Daniel.

"Well, it wasn't me who had the brilliant idea of killing the goose!" Emily yelled back.

They started to argue. They were still arguing the next day... and the day after that...

With no more golden eggs, soon Daniel and Emily were as poor as they had ever been. But now, instead of being happy, they were miserable.

Every morning, Daniel went down to the hen house to collect the eggs, muttering angrily to himself. And, as he picked the eggs out of the straw, his heart held a tiny hope that one of them might just be made of gold. But it never was.

The Leopard and the Sky God

Osebo the leopard had the best drum in all Africa. It was a mighty, musical drum that captured the beat of the forest, the pulse of the earth, the heat of the jungle. He could play it loud, play it soft, play it high, play it low. *Boom-di-di-boom* he played, even to the fireflies that danced at night.

Now everyone wanted Osebo's drum. Python wanted it. Elephant wanted it. Tortoise wanted it. But Osebo wouldn't let them have it.

"What about me?" asked Nyame, the Sky God. "Let me play it!"

"No," said Osebo. "It's *mine*."

Nyame watched and waited, but Osebo never let the drum out of his sight.

"I'll give a prize to the first animal who gets that drum for me," said Nyame.

"I'll try," said Python.

He slithered over to Osebo. "May I see it?" he asked.

"No!" roared Osebo, unsheathing his claws. Python slithered away.

"I'm not scared of Osebo," said Elephant.

He found Osebo playing his drum in a tree. "Show it to me!" trumpeted Elephant.

"Go away!" roared Osebo.

Elephant charged at the tree. He shook it till the leaves rained down, but Osebo stayed where he was.

"I couldn't do it,"
Elephant told Nyame.
"I'm sorry."

"Let me try," said
Tortoise. Now in those
days, Tortoise had no
shell, only a soft body.

The other animals
laughed. "You're no
match for Osebo," they scoffed.

"Wait and see," Tortoise said.

She found Osebo in his tree. "So Osebo!"
she began. "You thought you had the very
best drum in the whole jungle. But have you
seen Nyame's?"

"What are you talking about?" said Osebo.
"Nyame doesn't have a drum."

"Oh yes he does," taunted Tortoise. "It's
HUGE. It's so big, he can climb right
inside it."

"Well," said Osebo, "that's nothing. I can climb inside mine."

"I don't believe you," said Tortoise.

Osebo sprang down from the tree. He crawled inside his drum. "See!" he said.

Tortoise took the lid from Osebo's cooking pot and clapped it over the end of the drum. Then she rolled it along to the Sky God.

"I have it! I have it!" cried Nyame.

Osebo crawled out, dizzy and dazed. "You can keep it!" he gasped.

"And what would you like for your prize, little tortoise?" asked Nyame.

"I would like a shell on my body," Tortoise replied, "as hard as that drum, so that nothing can hurt me." And that is how Tortoise came to have her shell.

As for the Sky God, he loved his drum. When the weather is stormy, you can still hear him play, loud and soft, high and low...

The Firebird

Far away across the seas, there lived a rich and powerful King. His garden was studded with silver trees that blossomed with rubies, emeralds and diamonds. In the middle was the most precious tree of all, yielding apples of solid gold. One morning, he saw that a golden apple had been stolen.

"Find the thief!" the King begged his sons.

One by one, they waited up all night, only to fall asleep before dawn and wake to find another apple missing. At last, it was the turn of Prince Ivan, the youngest son.

He sang songs to keep
himself awake until the
sky grew so bright that he
thought the sun was waking.
But it was a beautiful bird,
its body glowing like hot coals,
feathers fluttering like flames. The
Firebird swooped down and snatched
a golden apple in its beak. Prince Ivan tried
to catch it, but its body was burning hot.

The prince rushed to tell his father what
had happened.

"I want that bird," said the King.

Prince Ivan rode out across the wintry land,
over frozen rivers and into a snow-filled forest.
Out of the darkness came a great silver wolf.

It sprang at Prince Ivan's horse, bringing it
to the ground with one bite to its neck.

The prince broke down and sobbed, before
turning on the wolf. "How will I find the

Firebird without a horse?" he demanded.

The silver wolf hung his head in shame. "I'm sorry," he said. "I was so hungry. Climb on my back. I'll take you to the Firebird."

Prince Ivan climbed on the wolf's back, nervously clinging to his fur, and the silver wolf sprang up, flying through the freezing air. They soared over snowy hills until night fell. The wolf landed softly just beyond the walls of a great castle.

Ivan caught sight of a flash of red feathers, as something flitted over the castle walls. "The Firebird!" he cried, reaching out to grab it. This time, the prince clung on, even as the fiery feathers scorched his hands.

"Don't kill me!" begged the Firebird.

"I'm not going to kill you," replied Ivan.

"My father wants to keep you in a golden cage."

"But I should fly free!" the bird pleaded.

Out of pity, Prince Ivan let her go. "Fly then," he said, quietly.

Yet, for a moment, the Firebird stayed where she was. "Take this feather," she said, passing him a long plume from her tail. "It will help you if you are ever in trouble." Then she flew away.

Prince Ivan turned to go when he heard laughter, like silver bells, coming from within the castle. Intrigued, he urged the wolf over the walls and they landed in a garden filled with rose trees and statues.

Twelve beautiful girls were dancing. They were joined by a princess, the most beautiful of them all.

"Please, run away while you can," she warned Ivan. "We are all trapped here. This castle belongs to Koschey the Deathless,  a terrible sorcerer. If he finds you, he will turn you to stone, just like the others," she added, pointing to the life-like statues.

Even as she spoke, the castle door opened. Koschey stormed out, a hundred hideous demons swirling around his scarlet cloak.

Ivan drew his sword and rushed at him, just as Koschey raised his arms. "You could never hope to hurt me," sneered Koschey. "I have hidden my heart outside my body."

Prince Ivan looked down in horror as he felt numbness spreading through him, an icy tingling that rushed up from his toes to his legs. "I'm turning to stone," he gasped.

Quickly, he pulled the Firebird's feather from his cloak.

It fluttered down and warmed him with its touch. Ivan could move once more.

"I know where his heart is," whispered the silver wolf. "Look in the box beneath the old tree stump." Then the wolf leaped at Koschey.

As they fought, Ivan ran to the tree stump. He pulled out the box, seized the egg inside and shook it. Koschey let out a scream as he was flung from side to side.

"Stop!" he cried. "Stop and I'll give you anything you want."

But Prince Ivan threw the egg into the air...

...and it crashed onto the ground, smashing into a thousand pieces. Koschey vanished, leaving only a wisp of black smoke in the air. All around, the statues came back to life.

"Come home with me," Ivan said to the princess, stretching out his hand to her.

Wordlessly she took it, and they climbed onto the silver wolf's back.

By evening, Ivan could see the lights of home. The King rushed out of the palace to welcome back his son. "I thought I'd never see you again," he cried.

Prince Ivan and the princess were soon married. And the Firebird still visited the King's garden, to feast on the golden apples. Only now, she was allowed to come and go in peace.

The Miller's Boy and the Mermaid

There was once a poor miller's boy who lived by a river. One day, he was cutting reeds when his knife slipped and sank — *splosh* — into the sparkling crystal water. "How will I get it back?" he wondered. A moment later, a mermaid with long, flowing hair appeared — holding a golden knife. "Is this yours?" she asked. The boy looked at it longingly, but shook his head.

The mermaid held up a silver knife. "How about this?" Again, the boy shook his head.

Finally, she held up a knife of rusty iron. The boy nodded. "That's mine, thank you!"

To his surprise, the mermaid laid all three knives on the bank before him. "Honesty deserves a reward," she told him, smiling, before diving back into the depths.

The miller's eyes lit up when he saw the knives and heard the boy's story. "Easy money," he chuckled, hurrying outside.

Splosh! Another knife sank into the water. "Oh no! How will I get it back?" he shouted.

Just as before, a mermaid appeared with a golden knife. "Is this yours?" she asked. The miller nodded, reaching out eagerly – but the mermaid snatched it away.

"There's no reward for lying," she snapped, sinking out of sight and leaving the miller empty-handed.

"I should have known," he sighed. "Honesty is always best."

The Enormous Turnip

Once upon a time, a long time ago, a farmer lived with his wife and son on a small farm. One morning, the farmer woke up, scratched his head and said, "I'm hungry. I think I'll go and dig up a turnip."

He studied his turnip patch. One turnip definitely looked a lot bigger than the others, with large, sprouting green leaves rising high above the earth. So he tugged at it. Nothing happened. He tugged at it a little more. STILL nothing happened. He bent down and *heaved* at the leaves. But the turnip wouldn't budge. "Are you all right, dear?" asked his wife.

"Not really," said the farmer. "I can't move this turnip."

So the wife hugged the farmer, who grabbed the turnip leaves and they both *heaved...* but the turnip wouldn't budge.

Their son saw them puffing and panting. "I'll help," he said.

The boy held his mother's skirt, she hugged the farmer who grabbed the turnip leaves and they all *heaved* together... but still, the turnip wouldn't budge.

"Woof!" barked their dog. "I'll help."

So the dog pulled the
boy's shirt, he held his
mother's skirt, she
hugged the farmer
who grabbed the
turnip leaves and they all *heaved...*
but still, the turnip wouldn't budge.

"Meeow!" said their cat. "I'll help."

So the cat tugged the dog's tail, the dog
pulled the boy's shirt, he held his mother's
skirt, she hugged the farmer who grabbed the
turnip leaves and they all *heaved...* but still, the
turnip wouldn't budge.

By now, everyone was very hot, very tired
and very grumpy. Just then, a little bird flew
past. "Tweet, tweet," she said. "I'll help."

"Let's try one last time," said the farmer, a
little breathlessly.

So the bird pecked the cat's tail, the cat
tugged the dog's tail, the dog pulled the boy's

shirt, he held his mother's skirt, she hugged the farmer who grabbed the turnip leaves and they all *heaved* and *heaved* and *heaved*...

And this time, slowly, slowly, the turnip began to move.

"It's HUGE!" cried the farmer.

"It's ENORMOUS!" cried his wife.

With a POP! the turnip flew out of the ground and everyone landed on top of each other, in a big, tangled heap.

"Goodness!" said the farmer. "Look at the size of that turnip. We'll be eating it for the rest of the year." And they did.

The Dragon Painter

Chang was a painter, but not just any old painter. He was the most talented animal painter in all of China. If he drew a rabbit, you would think its nose twitched. When he drew birds, you could almost hear them sing.

Now, it just so happened that the Emperor needed someone to decorate his new temple. "I want Chang," he decided.

Chang promised him a splendid mural with four dragons, one for each wall...

First, he drew a pearl-white dragon, breathing clouds of steam. It was perfect, except for one thing. Its eyes stared blankly out. Chang had left them unpainted.

"That's odd," thought the Emperor.

The next dragon was jade green, with a fierce, spiky face – and blank, white eyes. Then came a sleek, scarlet dragon and a golden dragon with a long, twisting tail – but both of them had blank eyes too.

Chang turned to the Emperor, and bowed. "Do you like your dragons, my lord?"

The Emperor nodded. "Magnificent!" he said. "But what about their eyes?"

"Dragons are magical beasts," said Chang. "If I paint their eyes, they will come to life."

"Piffle!" snapped the Emperor. "I order you to paint them in – at once!"

Chang was terrified, but he had to obey.
With a trembling hand, he began to dot in
the eyes. Thunder rumbled. As he finished,
there was an ear-splitting *CRASH!* A bolt of
lightning had shattered the roof.

The jade dragon blinked and lifted its head,
its spiky nose cracking part of the temple.
The pearl dragon yawned, sending out
clouds of burning
steam. Then, they
leaped off the walls
and flew through
the roof.

Before the red and gold dragons could follow, Chang seized his brush and painted strong chains around their necks. The dragons roared and rattled the chains, but they couldn't fly away.

So the Emperor was left with just two dragons on his temple walls. But they were the most incredible painted dragons in all of China.

The Elves and the Shoemaker

"I can't go on," sighed the old shoemaker in despair, one evening. "We have no more money." He was an honest, good man, who made beautiful shoes slowly and carefully, but his business was being ruined by the cobbler next door. This man sold hundreds of pairs of cheap shoes, and the shoemaker's customers all went to the new cobbler.

"What shall we do?" wept the shoemaker's wife. "You only have enough leather to make one last pair of shoes."

"I'll cut them out tonight, and make them tomorrow," said the shoemaker, and he climbed the stairs to bed with a heavy heart.

The next morning, a perfect pair of shoes complete with shining buckles stood on his workshop bench. Every stitch was exquisite.

"Look, wife!" squealed the shoemaker in amazement, putting them in the window. Instantly, a customer snapped them up. He paid so much that the shoemaker was able to buy enough leather for two more pairs. Again, he cut them out, planning to finish them the following morning.

And again, the magic happened. Two pairs of shoes appeared, with bows, laces, even pink heels... They were elegant, unique and exceptionally well-made.

"How is this happening?" wondered the shoemaker.

Every day, as he bought more leather, he found more wonderful shoes in the morning.

Soon he was rich again. His customers flocked back, fed up with the new cobbler's cheap shoes that let in the rain and fell to pieces after being worn once. The cobbler, furious, left town.

The shoemaker could hardly believe his good fortune. "We must stay awake and see who's helping us," he said to his wife.

That night, they hid in a corner of the workshop behind some coats and waited...

At midnight, two elves
clad in rags darted in.
They began to cut and
hammer and pierce
and stitch the leather
so skilfully and nimbly
with their little fingers that the shoemaker
gasped with astonishment.

"Those little men have made us wealthy,
and we must show them how grateful we
are," whispered his wife. "Their clothes are
so ragged, they must be freezing with cold.
I'll make them shirts and warm coats, fancy
waistcoats and breeches, and knit them each a
pair of socks. You can make them shoes."

The shoemaker and his wife spent all next
day making the tiny outfits, and left them
laid out on the workshop bench instead of the
pieces of leather. Then they hid again behind
the coats, to wait for the elves.

As midnight struck, the elves arrived, saw the clothes and quickly dressed themselves. They danced and skipped all over the workshop, singing in delight:

Now we are so fine to see

No more will we shoemakers be!

And they ran out of the shop, never to return.

Even without the elves, the shoemaker's business grew. He became famous throughout the land, because his shoes were the most sensational and magnificent ever seen, and he and his wife prospered to the end of their days.

The Ugly Duckling

In a clump of leaves by the edge of a pond, a mother duck sat impatiently on her eggs. She longed to glide on the water under the summer sun, but she had to wait until all her ducklings had hatched.

At last, the eggs began to crack and little heads poked out into the world. The other ducks gathered around to admire the new arrivals, but there was one egg – much larger than the rest – that still hadn't cracked.

"That's a turkey egg if ever I saw one," quacked an old duck. "Just leave it. You'll never teach that one to swim."

"I've waited this long, I can wait a little longer," said the mother duck.

Shortly after, there was a tap and a crack and the last duckling tumbled out of its shell. But was it a duckling? It was bigger than the others and very ugly.

"We'll soon see," thought the mother duck. She guided her ducklings down to the pond and one by one they jumped in. They disappeared under the water, then they all bobbed up again, floating with perfection.

"So you're not a turkey," the mother duck smiled. "You're just a big, ugly duckling."

She took her ducklings to the farmyard, where the Ugly Duckling was immediately picked on. The geese hissed at him. The hens pecked at him. The turkey puffed himself up like a ship under sail and chased after him with a fierce GOBBLE! GOBBLE! GOBBLE!

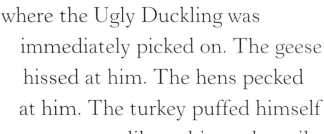

Even the Ugly Duckling's brothers and sisters teased him and his mother was too embarrassed to comfort him. The poor Ugly Duckling was so miserable, he ran away, flying over a fence and landing in a bush. Little birds darted up in fright. "They're scared of my ugly face," he thought sadly. He stumbled on to the great marsh where the wild ducks lived, and hid there all night long.

In the morning, the wild ducks flew up to look at him. "You're very ugly," they quacked, but they let him stay and drink the marsh water.

Suddenly: BANG! BANG! Shots rang in the air. Hunters were firing at the birds from all sides of the marsh. The wild ducks took off in panic as hunting dogs splashed through the water.

The Ugly Duckling hid his head
under his wing. SPLASH!
SPLASH! A massive dog
appeared above him,
his tongue lolling out
and his eyes glaring. He
opened his mouth wide,
flashing his sharp teeth,
then SPLASH! SPLASH! he
was off again.

"At least I'm too ugly to eat," trembled the
Ugly Duckling.

He kept low in the reeds for the rest of the
day, until the gun shots finally stopped and
the hunters left. Then he fled across fields
and meadows, buffeted by a stormy wind.

As night fell, he reached a ramshackle old
house. One hinge had come loose on the door,
which was slightly open, so the Ugly Duckling
squeezed inside to take shelter from the storm.

In the light of morning, the Ugly Duckling met a bossy hen and a curious cat, who lived in the house with a little old lady.

"Can I stay here?" asked the Ugly Duckling.

"Can you lay eggs?" clucked a hen.

"Can you arch your back or purr?" mewed the cat.

"I don't think so," said the Ugly Duckling.

"Then keep out of our way," they replied.

So the Ugly Duckling stayed in a dark corner. He thought of the fresh air and the sunlight, and had a sudden desire to glide over sparkling water.

"I don't belong here," he sighed to himself, and he went away to a large lake.

Every day, he swam and dived, but no animal would talk to him because of his ugliness. The weather grew colder and the forest leaves turned yellow and orange.

One evening, a flock of majestic white swans soared across the sunset, headed for warmer countries. The Ugly Duckling watched them in wonder. He had never seen anything so beautiful.

Winter was long and cold. Snow fell and the lake iced over. The Ugly Duckling barely survived, huddled beneath the reeds.

Eventually, spring came and he stretched out his wings. They were longer than before and stronger. Their powerful strokes lifted him out of the reeds and carried him to a large pond in a beautiful garden.

Three magnificent swans were already swimming in the pond. The Ugly Duckling hung his head in shame. These birds were sure to peck at him for his ugliness. But then he saw his reflection. Looking back at him from the water wasn't an ugly duckling at all. He had turned into a swan!

The other swans swam around him, stroking him with their beaks in welcome. As he stretched his neck in delight, several children ran up.

"Look, there's a new swan!" they cried. "And he's the most handsome of them all."

Rapunzel

Once upon a time, a young couple lived beside an enchanted garden. All kinds of herbs and plants grew there throughout the year. But no one ever set foot in it, for fear of the witch who owned it.

One bitter winter, the wife, who was expecting a baby, began to long for a taste of spring leaves. She craved them so much, she thought she would die without them. So, bravely, her husband entered the garden. He had picked just one leaf, of a plant named Rapunzel, when a shout rang out.

"Stop!"

It was the witch. "How dare you steal my plants? You will pay with your life."

"S-s-sorry," he stammered. "Please, it was for my wife, she is expecting a baby."

"A baby?" muttered the witch. "Well, in that case, take all you want. In exchange, I will take the child."

No one dared disobey the witch. With heavy hearts, the couple waited... The baby, when she came, was a beautiful, rosy-cheeked girl. They had just wrapped her in a blanket when the witch tapped at the door.

"I'll call her Rapunzel," she cackled, as she took her away, "in memory of our bargain."

So Rapunzel grew up with the witch, who guarded her jealously. When she was twelve, the witch locked her in a tower with no door. The only way in or out was to climb the outside, but the walls of the tower were as slippery as glass.

Rapunzel had long golden hair which grew and grew, and was never cut. When the witch visited, she would call up: "Rapunzel, Rapunzel, let down your hair." Then Rapunzel would let her hair tumble down to the ground, and the witch would climb up it.

One day, a prince was riding by the tower when he saw Rapunzel. She was so beautiful, he lost his heart to her in an instant. And Rapunzel, who had never seen a man before, was equally charmed. Quickly, she let down her hair. Boldly, the prince climbed up. They talked and laughed and, by sunset, they had vowed to marry.

"You must go before the witch finds you," warned Rapunzel. "Or she'll kill you."

"I'll be back with a rope ladder," promised the prince. "And we'll escape together!"

But when the witch returned, she knew at once. "A man has been here," she spat. "Who is he?"

Rapunzel pressed her lips firmly together.

"Never mind, I'll find out!" snarled the witch. She chopped off Rapunzel's beautiful hair and locked her in a cupboard. And then she waited...

Before long, there came a whisper. "Rapunzel, Rapunzel, let down your hair."

The golden tresses tumbled down and the prince climbed up – only to find the witch holding them at the other end.

"You'll never see your darling again," she cackled, trying to push him out of the window.

"No," cried the prince, jerking the hair...

The witch, who was still clutching it tightly, was thrown off balance. She teetered for a moment, then fell through the window. There was a loud shriek – and a sudden silence.

"Well, that's the end of her," sighed the prince, looking around. "Rapunzel?"

"Here," came a soft voice. The prince unlocked the cupboard, and she rushed into his arms.

"We're free," he said, smiling. "Now we can climb down my rope ladder and live happily ever after."

And they did.

The Boy Who Cried Wolf

Looking after sheep has never been the most exciting job in the world. But it wasn't until Nico sat on a cold, windy mountainside, and listened to the sound of twenty-eight sheep, nibbling at some grass, that he realized just how unexciting it could be.

He tried whistling, and discovered he couldn't whistle. He tried chewing a piece of straw – it tasted horrible. There was nothing he could do to change the fact that watching over sheep was dull.

To make matters worse, he could hear sounds drifting up from his village in the valley – the sounds of his friends, shouting, singing and laughing. They were all playing together, while he was sitting on the top of a mountain with a hungry belly, a cold wind and twenty-eight sheep for company.

As the day went on, Nico felt more and more sorry for himself, and then a slow, sneaky smile spread across his face.

He jumped up and started running down the mountain.

"WOLF!" he shouted. "There's a WOLF! A wolf is attacking the sheep!"

The villagers heard him yelling, and dropped what they were doing at once.

Grabbing brooms and sticks, they all came scrambling up the mountain. When they got to the top, they were red-faced and sweating, heaving, puffing and panting, but they were ready to fight the wolf.

All they saw was a small boy, laughing and clapping his hands with glee.

"Tricked you!" he said. "I've never seen anything so funny in my whole life!"

"It's not funny at all," said the baker.

"That's because you couldn't see yourself running up the mountain!" said Nico.

The villagers were not impressed. Grumbling loudly, they strode back down to the village.

The next day, Nico was sitting on top of the mountain again, with his herd of sheep, feeling utterly bored.

"I shouldn't," he thought. "I really shouldn't. I definitely shouldn't... WOLF!" he shouted, unable to help himself.

"WOLF!" he yelled, at the top of his lungs. "It's really here! It's enormous! Help!"

Not all of the villagers came running this time, but most of them did, just in case. Again, they brought their mops and brooms and sticks to scare off the big bad...

...oh.

There was no wolf. When they finally got to the top, all they saw was the herd of sheep, and Nico.

This time he was laughing even harder. "I can't believe you believed me!" he said. "That was so funny!"

"It wasn't funny AT ALL," said the villagers, scowling at him. And they stomped off down the side of the mountain.

On the third day, Nico was back on the mountain. "There's just nothing to do here," he thought, "except look at the sheep, and the wolf... hold on. Wolf? WOLF!"

For this time there really was a wolf. It leaped out of a clump of trees, and ran towards the sheep with a murderous glint in its eye.

"WOLF! WOLF! WOLFFFF!" Nico yelled, running down the mountainside.

"WOLF!" he screamed, as he ran around the village square.

"Come quickly! Help me! HELP!"

Not one of the villagers moved. The teacher slowly turned over a page of his book. The butcher rolled some sausages. The baker iced a small bun.

"HELP!" Nico begged the villagers. "Please, help!" But they all ignored him, and so, eventually, Nico had to walk back up the mountain alone. He was dreading what he would find when he got to the top. Sure  enough, the wolf had done its worst.

It had killed most of the sheep, while the others had run away. Nico sat down, put his head in his hands, and cried.

When night fell, some of the villagers went to look for Nico, and found the terrible scene.

"Our sheep!" they said. "Our poor sheep!"

"Why didn't you help me?" Nico asked, in a small voice. But he already knew the answer.

"You always lied to us, so we didn't believe you," they replied.

"I've learned my lesson," said Nico. "I'll never lie again."

How Elephants Lost Their Wings

O nce upon a time, elephants could fly.
They flew everywhere on four fluttering,
leafy, feathery wings. They
stuck out their trunks
and lifted their legs and
flapped and flapped,
shouting, "Look at
me! I'm higher than
the trees!"

They soared up and up, circled the sun,
then dived back down to the ground. They
could loop the loop, twizzle and twirl, fly in
a straight line and end with a swirl. To be an
elephant was to fly.

"We love it," they would sigh.

"These elephants are wonderful," agreed the gods, who sailed through the sky on their backs. "We love to travel by elephant. It's so majestic and magnificent..."

But there was a problem. The elephants were noisy. They trumpeted, and crowed like roosters. "Cock-a-doodle-doo!" they boomed across the sky.

Trees and houses shook below them. They collided with trees and snapped them. They crash-landed on houses and flattened them. Wherever the elephants flew, they left chaos and destruction behind.

Trees were bent and broken. Houses were smashed to smithereens. "We must stop them from flying," said the gods, sadly, and thought of a trick. "Dear elephants," they said. "You are all invited to a feast."

Elephant after elephant came to the fruity feast. They slurped and guzzled. They chomped and gobbled. They ate to their heart's content. And when at last they had finished the meal, they lay down and fell fast asleep.

This was the moment the gods had been waiting for. As the elephants snored, they crept up and stole their wings.

They gave some to the peacocks, to wear as splendid tails. They stuck some on the banana trees, giving them magnificent green leaves.

As for the elephants... they were furious. "Where are our wings?" they blasted when they woke.

"Gone," replied the gods. "Gone forever."

The elephants shouted and they stomped. They stormed along the ground until the whole jungle quaked. But there was nothing they could do. They had lost their wings and would never fly again.

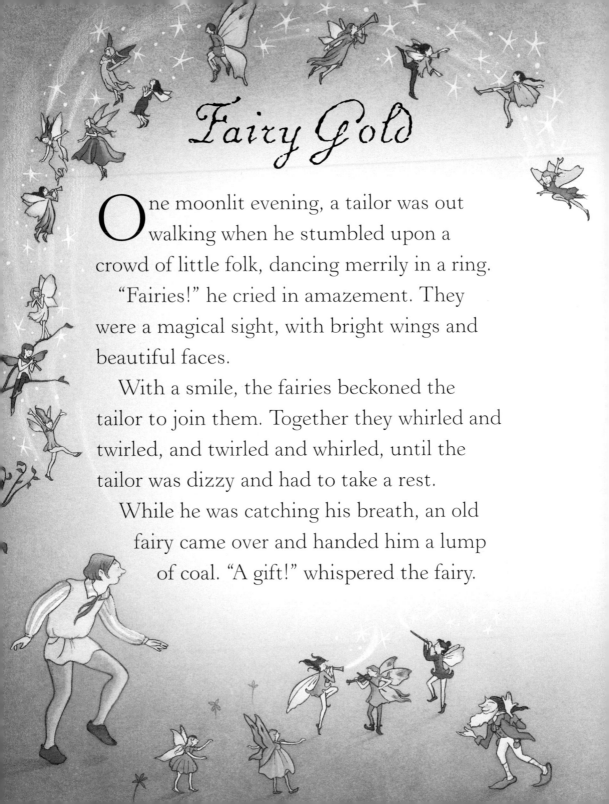

Fairy Gold

One moonlit evening, a tailor was out walking when he stumbled upon a crowd of little folk, dancing merrily in a ring.

"Fairies!" he cried in amazement. They were a magical sight, with bright wings and beautiful faces.

With a smile, the fairies beckoned the tailor to join them. Together they whirled and twirled, and twirled and whirled, until the tailor was dizzy and had to take a rest.

While he was catching his breath, an old fairy came over and handed him a lump of coal. "A gift!" whispered the fairy.

"How odd," thought the tailor, but he took it anyway. Then he yawned and closed his eyes – and when he opened them again, it was morning.

The fairies had gone, and his hand felt strangely heavy... He looked down. Instead of coal, he was holding a gleaming lump of gold!

"I'm rich," he chuckled. He was about to run home to show everyone when a thought struck him. "I wonder if I can get more?"

The tailor waited all day. At dusk, the fairies reappeared. Again, he joined in the dancing, and again, the old fairy handed him a lump of coal. He went to sleep dreaming of riches.

When he woke, he looked eagerly at his hands – only to find his fingers black and sooty. "Nooo!" he wailed. He was holding two lumps of coal. "If only I hadn't been so greedy," he sighed. But it was too late – his fortune had gone for good.

The Emperor and the Nightingale

This is a story about an Emperor, who ruled over all of China. His palace was the most beautiful in the world, with gardens that stretched as far as the eye could see. Even the Emperor himself didn't know where they ended. These gardens were full of beautiful flowers and tinkling bells. But the most beautiful sound by far was the nightingale's song.

Her lofty melody soared to the skies like a silver ribbon of sound. The Emperor, shut up in his precious palace, had never heard her sing.

One day, as he sat reading in his library, he came across a book about the marvels in his palace. He smiled as he read it, until he came across this line...

The nightingale is the most beautiful of all.

"What's this?" cried the Emperor. "I've never heard of this creature. Bring her to me!" he ordered his servants.

They ran around the palace, even looking up in the attics and down in the cellars, but they could not find her anywhere.

"Perhaps it's made up?" they said, bowing low before the Emperor.

"Nonsense," he snapped. "Bring her to me by supper or I'll have you all trampled on."

They rushed into the garden, peering into ponds and scrambling through bushes.

"What are you looking for?" asked the gardener.

"Something called a nightingale," sighed the servants.

The gardener smiled. "Come with me."

He led them to a little brown bird in a tree.

"That's a nightingale?" they asked. "That drab piece of nothing?"

"Wait," said the gardener, as if sharing a secret. Then the nightingale began to sing. Her sweet song pierced the air. The palace servants began to clap.

"Please come with us," they said. "The
Emperor wants to hear you sing."

"My song sounds best in the open air,"
said the bird. "But I will come if the Emperor
wishes it."

The nightingale sang so sweetly
for the Emperor that tears
came to his eyes, then
rolled down his cheeks.
The Emperor wanted the
nightingale by him always
and ordered her a golden
cage. Soon, she was
famous across the land.
Then a package arrived from
the Emperor of Japan. Inside was a clockwork
nightingale, covered in glittering jewels.

When a servant wound her up, she sang –
a tinkling little tune.

Everyone watched in wonder.

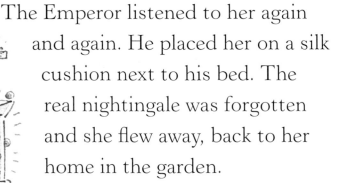

The Emperor listened to her again and again. He placed her on a silk cushion next to his bed. The real nightingale was forgotten and she flew away, back to her home in the garden.

But one evening, as the Emperor lay in bed, something inside the clockwork nightingale went *whizz, whir-r-r, clunk*. And the music stopped. Nothing could be done to fix her. The Emperor remembered his little brown nightingale and wanted her again, but she could not be found.

A year passed and the Emperor lay very ill in bed. Everyone expected each breath to be his last. The Emperor looked at the clockwork bird. "I want music," he gasped. "Please." But the bird could not sing.

Death hovered over the Emperor and he closed his eyes. Then, from the window, came the lilting notes of the nightingale. She sang of white roses and fresh, wet grass, of the elder-tree and the quiet of the churchyard. And Death floated out through the window in the form of a cold, white mist.

The nightingale sang the Emperor to sleep. When he awoke, he was strong and well again.

"Stay with me always," he said to the nightingale. "You may sing when it pleases you and I'll break the clockwork bird into a thousand pieces."

"Don't do that," said the nightingale. "The bird served you as best it could. I cannot live in the palace, but I will sit in a bough outside your window and build my nest there."

And for the rest of his days, the Emperor would lean out of his window and smile to hear the nightingale's song.

The Rabbit's Tale

Rabbit was fed up. His home was simply too small. "It's so cramped," he moaned. "Living here, I'm squished and I'm squashed at every turn. I need more room."

After grumbling to himself for a while, he perked up. "I know!" he said. "I'll go and see Owl. He's wise. He'll be able to help."

"My home is too small,"
he called to Owl, who sat
watching the world from his tree.

"Hmm..." said Owl. "And you want
to make it bigger." He thought for a moment
and then declared, "You must ask all your
brothers and sisters to stay."

"Really?" said Rabbit. "Do you think that
will help?"

"Oh yes," Owl nodded. "That should do it."

Rabbit was baffled but he did as Owl said.

That afternoon, all his brothers and sisters
moved in. It was a tight squeeze.

Rabbit went straight back to Owl. "I asked
all my brothers and sisters," he told him, "and
now there's less room. What can I do?"

Owl smiled. "Invite all your friends, too."

"Really?" said Rabbit again,
feeling even more confused.

"Oh yes," said Owl.

So Rabbit went to see all of his friends and asked them to stay. One by one, they all trooped into his house.

Rabbit stood in the middle of his living room and gazed around in dismay. "This is ridiculous!" he thought. "I don't have room to move."

And he squeezed through the crowds and ran back to Owl.

"Help!" he shouted. "I took your advice and now there's no room for me."

"Don't panic," said Owl, in a calm voice. "Just tell them it's time to go home."

So Rabbit went back and told his brothers and sisters and all his friends that it was time to leave.

"Thanks for having us," they called as they trooped out again.

As his last friend left, Rabbit looked around his empty house. It felt enormous. He leaped in the air in delight.

"My home is huge!" he cried. "Thank you Owl. What a wise old bird you are."

The Magic Pear Tree

A monk, dressed in ragged robes, gazed hungrily around the market. His eyes alighted on a cart, laden with plump, golden pears.

"I have no money," the monk said to the fruit-seller. "I gave up everything I had for God. But now I am hungry. Please," he begged, "may I have one pear?"

"No," said the fruit-seller shortly. "If you can't pay me any money, I'm not interested. GO AWAY!"

"But you have so many pears," said the tea-seller at the next cart along. "Surely you could give him just one?"

"I said no, and I meant it," retorted the fruit-seller.

"Then I'll buy him one myself," the tea-seller said.

He paid for the pear and handed it to the monk, who ate it greedily, until only the seeds were left. Bending down, he buried them in the ground.

"A little water, if you please?" he said to the tea-seller.

The monk poured hot water onto the seeds. Everyone gathered to watch.

"Aaah!" said the crowd, as the seeds turned into a shoot.

"Oooh!" said the crowd, as the shoot turned into a tree.

"Amazing!" cried the crowd, as the tree sprouted luscious golden pears, dripping from every branch.

"Now," said the monk. "I invite you all to have one of my pears."

Everyone took one of the pears, even the fruit-seller. While the crowd was busy eating, the monk picked up a hatchet and quietly chopped down the tree. Then he walked away.

The fruit-seller turned around. He gasped. All his pears had gone, and his wooden cart was chopped to pieces.

"It was a trick!" he wailed. "Those pears were mine. The monk used magic to turn my cart into the tree."

But the crowd only laughed. "Maybe next time," they said, "you'll be quicker to share."

The Little Mermaid

Far beneath the waves lived a little mermaid. She was the Sea King's daughter, the youngest of six beautiful sisters, all with flowing hair and eyes as blue as the deepest waters. Their home was a coral palace, where fishes flitted through great halls.

Outside the palace was a garden, with flaming red and deep-blue trees growing in soil of the finest sand. Each princess had her own plot, where she could plant whatever she liked. One of them made a flower bed shaped like a whale. The youngest made hers as round as the sun, and there she grew only scarlet flowers, as rosy red as the sun itself.

She was a strange child, quiet and wistful.

While her sisters decorated their gardens with all sorts of treasures rescued from sunken ships, the little mermaid had only one white marble statue, of a handsome boy. Nothing gave her more pleasure than hearing about the land above the waves.

"When you get to be fifteen," her grandmother said, "you will be allowed to rise up out of the ocean and sit on the rocks in the moonlight, to watch the ships sailing by."

As each sister turned fifteen, they swam up to the surface. Back they came, with stories of sun, sky – and people. The little mermaid listened longingly.

Once, after a storm, she'd rescued a human prince from drowning. She never forgot him.

"One day," she vowed, "I'll find my prince."

On her fifteenth birthday, her grandmother combed her flowing hair, and let oysters attach themselves to her tail.

"Ow!" cried the little mermaid, but her grandmother replied, "Be still. Don't you want to look beautiful for your birthday?"

"Do humans think we are beautiful?"

"Humans!" scoffed the grandmother. "They don't have tails like us, but ugly legs instead."

At last, her grandmother finished and the mermaid rose up through the water as light and sparkling as a bubble. The sun had just gone down when her head rose above the surface, but the clouds still shone, golden and rosy-pink. The air was mild and fresh and the sea unruffled.

In front of her lay a great three-masted ship, lively with music and singing, and brightly-lit by hundreds of lanterns.

The little mermaid swam up to the window of the main cabin, gazing at the crowd of brilliantly dressed people within. The most handsome of all was a young prince with big dark eyes. "My prince!" she thought, and love for him flooded her whole heart.

Sighing, she dived back down to the bottom of the sea and her father's palace, but many evenings and most mornings after that, she swam up to where his palace stood, desperate for just a glimpse of him.

One night, her father held a court ball. Amidst the singing and dancing, the little mermaid slipped away to sit sadly in her garden. All she could think of was the prince.

"If I had legs," she thought, "I could be with him forever." So she decided to visit the sea witch, to ask for her help. Raging whirlpools blocked the way and branches of worms grabbed at her hair. The little mermaid was terrified and nearly turned back, but she remembered the prince and summoned her courage. Binding her hair tightly to her head, she darted through the water like a fish.

In a muddy clearing, she found the sea witch, feeding toads.

"I know exactly what you want, foolish thing," said the sea witch. "You want two legs so you can walk about like a human creature, and have the young prince fall in love with you."

At this, she gave a loud, cackling laugh.

"Well, I can make a potion, but if I give you legs, every step will stab you like a sword. You will lose your voice. You can never be a mermaid again," she warned.

"What will I have left?" asked the little mermaid.

"Your beauty," replied the witch. "But beware, if the prince doesn't love you back, you will die. Do you still want the potion?"

"Yes," the little mermaid said, thinking of the prince, though her voice trembled.

She swallowed the potion the witch poured for her and fell instantly asleep. When she awoke, she was lying on the beach and her prince was bending over her.

"Who are you?" he asked, but she had no voice and couldn't utter a word.

"*I love you,*" said her eyes.

"You remind me of a maiden I dreamed of when I nearly drowned," said the prince. "Come! Walk with me to my castle."

Every step was agony.

The little mermaid stayed with him, but he loved her as if she were only a younger sister or a pet. Once, walking by the sea she saw her own sisters.

"Come back," they chorused, stretching out their arms, but the little mermaid knew she couldn't return to her old life.

After a time, the prince told her he was to be married. "My princess looks a little like you," he smiled. "Aren't you happy for me?"

The little mermaid's heart broke at his words. She went to the shore, where she saw her sisters, all with short hair.

"We gave the sea witch our hair for a magic knife," they called. "If you just kill the prince, you can be a mermaid again."

The little mermaid took the knife from them, but then she flung it into the foaming waves. "I could never hurt my prince," she thought. "I still love him..."

With that, she slipped into the sea, and disappeared forever.

The Twelve Dancing Princesses

Once, a King had twelve beautiful, lively daughters. Each evening, he locked them in a tower to keep them safe. Yet every morning their shoes were worn to shreds, as though they'd been dancing through the night. They had to have new shoes every single day.

The King couldn't understand it. "Any man," he announced, "who discovers where the princesses go, may marry whichever he likes. But any man who tries and fails, will instantly have his head chopped off."

A succession of brave, rich, clever men followed each other to the princesses' tower. One after the other, each man was beheaded. The King was in despair... and then a poor soldier came along to try his luck.

Just before he entered the tower, he met an old woman, who felt sorry for him. Liking his looks, she warned, "Don't drink the cocoa they offer you. Pretend to go straight to sleep. And take this invisibility cloak so you can follow them."

When the eldest princess gave the soldier a mug of cocoa, he cunningly poured it away and never tasted a drop. Then he yawned, lay down and shut his eyes, leaving them open just a crack. The youngest princess, he thought, was the loveliest.

She, in her turn, was sad to think this
handsome soldier would soon die. The soldier
watched the girls put on sparkling jewels and
slip into new dancing
shoes. Then he saw
them open a trapdoor
and disappear down
a secret staircase.

Hastily, the soldier
threw on the invisibility cloak and ran to join

them. Beyond the stairs was
an avenue of trees, their
leaves sprinkled with gold and
glittering with diamonds. He
snapped off a branch to show
the King, and the youngest
princess turned back, startled.

"There's no one there," said
her older sister. "That soldier
was fast asleep."

On they walked, the soldier following, until they reached a lake. Here, twelve boats were waiting, each with a prince at the helm.

The sisters jumped aboard and were rowed to a glorious castle. There, they danced the night away, till the soles of their shoes were worn right through. At dawn, they were rowed back home.

After breakfast, the soldier went to report to the King.

"Failed, I suppose," said the King, with a shrug. "Off with his head!"

"Not at all, Sire," said the soldier. "Would you please call the princesses here?"

He produced the shimmering branch he'd
broken from the trees, and told the King
what he had seen. Blushing, the princesses
confessed everything.

True to his word, the King offered one of
his daughters in marriage. The soldier chose
the youngest, who was pleased to accept.
Their wedding was held that very day and the
dancing lasted a week.

Baba Yaga

In a far flung corner of Old Russia lived a little girl called Vasilisa. Her mother had died when Vasilisa was very young, but before she died, she gave her daughter a wooden doll.

"If you are ever in danger," her mother said, "give this doll food and water, and she will help you."

A few years later, Vasilisa's father married again. His new wife was a wicked woman who didn't want a stepdaughter, but she bided her time. She watched and waited.

Then one day, Vasilisa's father announced he had to go away for a whole day, to the market town over the mountains.

"Take care of my daughter

while I am gone," he told his new wife.

"I will, I will," his wife replied. But as soon as he'd left, she called for Vasilisa.

"We have no more candles," she said. "Tonight we will be in darkness. I need you to go to Baba Yaga's hut in the forest to get us a light."

"But... Baba Yaga is a witch!" thought Vasilisa. "A terrifying, child-eating witch."

She crept outside and, with trembling hands, took her doll from her pocket. The time had come to ask for help.

She fed her doll some bread. She gave her sips of water. The little doll's eyes lit up like stars.

"Little doll, little doll," whispered Vasilisa. "Stepmother is sending me to Baba Yaga's hut.

She eats children as if they were chickens.
What should I do? Please, help me!"

"Go," said the doll. "I shall protect you.
Take some bread for Baba Yaga's dog. Take
some meat for Baba Yaga's cat. You will come
to no harm."

Vasilisa packed a loaf of bread and slices of
meat and set off through the forest. Soon, a
wild wind began to blow. The trees
creaked. Their branches
groaned. Vasilisa heard a
thump, thump, thump and
a *swish, swish, swish.* She
looked up to see Baba
Yaga flying past in her
magic pot. The witch
pushed herself along with a
wooden spoon and wiped away
her tracks with a long wooden broom.

Twisting and turning between the trees,

Vasilisa stumbled after the
flying witch. At last, she
came to a little hut, which
stood high off the ground
on chicken's legs.

The little doll
whispered in Vasilisa's ear
and Vasilisa called out, "Hut,
oh hut, turn around, twirl your
feet upon the ground."

The hut twirled around on its scaly legs. It
winked at Vasilisa with window-like eyes and
cried, "I can dance, I can see, a little girl in
front of me."

Baba Yaga leaped out of the hut. "What
have we here?" she cackled.

She smiled at Vasilisa – a dreadful smile,
for her mouth was full of iron teeth.

Her hair was greasy. Her face was warty.
Her nose reached down to her chin.

"Stepmother sent me to ask for a light," said Vasilisa, her voice trembling with fear.

"I'll help you," croaked Baba Yaga. "But first you must sweep my floor." She hustled Vasilisa into the hut and closed the door behind her.

"Make me a huge crackling fire," Baba Yaga called to her maid, her voice like grating stones. "I'm going to eat that girl for lunch."

Inside the hut, Vasilisa could hear every word. She sat down and began to cry.

"I'll help you," purred Baba Yaga's cat. "But what will you give me in return?"

Vasilisa held out the slices of meat and the cat gobbled them up.

"You must run away, as fast as you can," whispered the cat. "But first take Baba Yaga's mirror and comb." The cat handed them over. "When you hear Baba Yaga coming, throw down the mirror. And if she keeps on coming, throw down the comb."

"Thank you," said Vasilisa, wiping away her tears. She took the comb and the mirror and ran from the hut... where Baba Yaga's big black dog was waiting for her.

It snarled. It growled. It showed sharp pointed teeth.

Vasilisa threw the dog the bread and it fell upon the loaf. "Keep running," it barked between mouthfuls. "Keep running."

Back came Baba Yaga. "Are you sweeping, little girl?" she called.

"Yesssss, I'm sweeping," hissed the cat.

"That is not the child's voice!" cried Baba Yaga. She leaped into the hut. "Where's the girl?" she screamed at the cat.

"I helped her escape," said the cat, still licking the meat from its paws. "After all, she gave me food. In all the time I've served you, you've never even given me a morsel to eat."

Baba Yaga raced out to her dog. "Why didn't you stop her?" she screeched.

"I've served you for a long time," said the dog, still licking crumbs from its mouth. "But you've never given me food. That girl gave me bread to eat."

Baba Yaga turned red with rage. She whistled through her ancient lips and her magic pot sped towards her. She snapped her fingers, and her spoon and her broom shot into her hands. Then away she flew. *Thump, thump, thump* went the spoon. *Swish, swish, swish* went the broom.

Vasilisa heard her coming.

"Throw down the mirror!" cried the little doll. Vasilisa threw it behind her, and turned to see the mirror had become a wide, wide river.

"Curses!" cried Baba Yaga. She bent her bony body and drank and drank and drank.

When she had drunk the whole river she took to her pot again. *Thump, thump, thump* went the spoon. *Swish, swish, swish* went the broom.

Vasilisa heard her coming.

"Throw down the comb!" cried the doll. Vasilisa threw the comb behind her. With a rumbling roar, the ground split, and Vasilisa turned to see a craggy mountain rising up to the sky.

"Curses!" cried Baba Yaga. She bent down and began to chew through the mountain. *Crunch, crunch, crunch* went her iron teeth. But they were rusty from drinking the wide, wide river and, one by one, they snapped.

Baba Yaga shook her fist. She was defeated by her own magic. The mountain was too high to fly over. It was time to turn back.

Vasilisa heard the *thump!* of the spoon and the *swish!* of the broom growing fainter and fainter. But she didn't stop running until she reached home.

Her father rushed out to meet her. "Where have you been?" he asked.

"Stepmother sent me to Baba Yaga's hut," Vasilisa panted, "and she tried to eat me."

"Then it's time your stepmother left," said her father.

He threw the wicked woman out of the house, and she was never seen again. As for Vasilisa, she grew up to be wise and beautiful... and the wife of the Tsar himself. But that is another story.

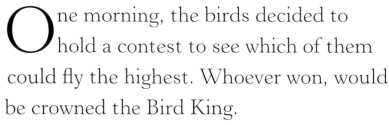

The Bird King

One morning, the birds decided to hold a contest to see which of them could fly the highest. Whoever won, would be crowned the Bird King.

"Eagle will win," said the other birds. "He's so majestic and strong."

"Why should the biggest and the strongest be the winner?" thought Wren, and he was still thinking that when the contest began.

With a drumroll from Woodpecker, hammering his beak on a tree, the birds were off. One by one, they took to the air in a flurry of whirring wings.

Grouse was first to turn back, his body too heavy for his stumpy wings. "Go-back, go-back, go-back," he called, diving down to the ground.

Soon, only two
birds were left, the
mighty eagle and the
tiny wren. Eagle soared
higher and higher, scything
circles through the air. Wren
flew straight up, little wings
frantically fluttering.

"I can't last much longer..." he thought.
"It's time, now, to try my trick." And he
drifted down, landing gently on Eagle's back.

Eagle looked around the sky and thought he
was alone in the airy blue. "I'm the winner!"
he announced. "I'm King!"

At that moment, Wren flew off his back and
up into the sky again. "No! *I'm* the winner!"
he cried. "*I'm* the King!"

There was nothing Eagle could do. Too exhausted to fly further, he glided back to the ground on his aching wings. And that very day, in a ceremony attended by all the birds, the tiny wren was crowned the Bird King.

Wren gave Eagle a secret smile. "I couldn't have done it without you," he said.

"No," replied Eagle. "You used *my* strength."

"And *my* brains," laughed Wren.

Rumpelstiltskin

Once upon a time, there was a boastful miller who had a beautiful daughter. One day, the King himself rode through their village. He stopped and stared at the miller's daughter, captivated by her beauty.

The miller couldn't help himself. He went up to the King and whispered, "Not only is she beautiful, she can spin straw into gold."

Without another word, the King swung the miller's daughter up in the saddle behind him. Then he rode off with her to his castle, leading her up a twisting turret to a little room stuffed with straw.

"Get to work at once," he said. "By morning I want all this straw turned to gold. Otherwise, you shall die."

The miller's daughter sat down and wept. "I don't know how to spin straw into gold," she sobbed. "No one does."

"Oh really?" came a voice at the window. The miller's daughter looked up. There, riding on a wooden spoon, was the strangest little man she'd ever seen.

"I'll do it for you," he rasped, jumping into the room. "But what will you give me in return?"

"My necklace," said the miller's daughter.

"It's a deal," cackled the strange little man. He sat down at the spinning wheel and began.

Whir, *whir*, *whir* went the
wheel, and bobbin by
bobbin, the straw
was spun into gold.
Morning came
and the little
man had gone,
leaving the gold behind
him. When the King came in, his eyes lit up
in delight.

"Come with me," he said. This time he led
the miller's daughter to a much bigger room.
Once again, it was stuffed with straw. "Turn
the straw to gold by morning," he said, "or
tomorrow, you shall die."

With tears in her eyes, the miller's daughter
rushed to the window. The strange little man
was there again. "What will you give me if I
help you this time?" he asked.

"The ring on my finger," she replied.

The strange little man sat down and began to spin. *Whir, whir, whir* went the wheel, turning the straw to gold.

By morning he had vanished, leaving the gold behind him.

"This is wonderful," said the King. "But I need *more*." He showed the miller's daughter to the largest room of all, with straw piled almost to the ceiling. "Spin this too, all through the night," said the King. "If you succeed, you shall be my wife."

That night, the little man appeared for the third time. "What will you give me if I spin again?" he asked.

"I have nothing left to give," replied the miller's daughter.

"Then promise me this," said the little man. "When you are Queen, you will give me your firstborn child."

The miller's daughter agreed. "He's sure to forget," she whispered to herself.

When the King came in the next morning, he found there was enough gold to last him all his life. The following day, the miller's daughter became his wife.

A year passed, and the Queen gave birth to

a baby boy, whom she loved more than her own life. She had forgotten all about the strange little man, until, one snowy night, he came knocking at her window.

"Give me what you promised," he said, staring at the baby.

"No! No!" cried the Queen. "Take anything you want, but not my baby."

The little man frowned, but at last he took pity on her. "I'll give you three days," he said. "If you can discover my name in that time, you may keep your child."

The Queen lay awake through the night, trying to remember every name she had ever heard. When the little man came the next evening, she said, "Is it James? Is it Peter? Is it John?"

But every time the little man shook his head and declared, "That is not my name."

The next day the Queen journeyed far and wide, asking everyone she met their name.

That night, she recalled all the peculiar names she had learned.

"Is your name Sheepshanks? Is it Shortribs? Is it Laceleg?" she asked.

But each time, the little man shook his head and said, "That is not my name."

On the third day, the Queen set off again, but could not find any new names. She came home in despair.

"Something strange happened to me today," said the King, at supper. "I went hunting, deep in the forest and there I saw a little house. Outside, around a fire, a funny little man was leaping about and singing the oddest song. It went:

Today I bake, tomorrow brew,
The next I'll do the same.
Ha! Glad I am that no one knew
That Rumpelstiltskin is my name!

The Queen smiled as she heard the story, but said nothing.

When the little man came that night, she said at first, "Is your name Pegleg? Is it..." she paused, "...Zebedee?"

"No, no, no!" laughed the little man, jumping about the room in excitement.

"Perhaps," said the Queen, after an even longer pause, "your name is Rumpelstiltskin?"

"How did you know that?" he cried, shaking his fist at her, his eyes filled with tears of rage.

Then he leaped on his spoon, burst through the wall, and was never seen again.

Brer Rabbit and the Briar Patch

Now, there was once a mischievous creature called Brer Rabbit who had an old enemy, Brer Fox. Those two were always fighting and trying to trick each other.

"He's a rascally rabbit," thought Brer Fox. "It's time I taught him a lesson," and he decided to set a trap. He took a long rope, tied it to a tree, looped the other end and laid that on the ground. Then he covered it with leaves.

Lippety-clippety, clippety-lippety. Along came Brer Rabbit, sassy and swaggering, as if he were the king of the world.

Brer Fox chuckled and lay low in the
bushes, neatly hidden from view.

Brer Rabbit bounded along until...
TWANG! went the trap, the rope snapping
around his ankle.

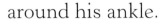

"Uh oh!" said
Brer Rabbit.
He wriggled.
He jiggled.
He twisted and turned,
he writhed and squirmed
but there was no getting
out of that trap. Brer
Rabbit was stuck fast
and he knew it.

Brer Fox watched it all
with a grin and then he strutted out from
the bushes.

"Got you!" he cried. "I've got you and now
I'm going to gobble you up!"

He licked his chops.

"Hurray!" cried Brer Rabbit.

"Hurray?" said Brer Fox. "You mean you *want* me to eat you?"

"Oh yes!" sang Brer Rabbit. "Please eat me. Fry me, boil me, bake me in a pie. But whatever you do, please, please, *please*, don't throw me in the briar patch."

"What's wrong with the briar patch?" asked Brer Fox.

"It's full of horrible, scratchy, prickly thorns. Don't put me in there, Brer Fox. Those thorns will tear me to pieces."

"Then that's exactly what I'll do," grinned Brer Fox.

He grabbed Brer Rabbit by the ears. He hurled him through the air.

Brer Rabbit whizzed around like a whirligig and landed – SPLAT – right in the middle of the briar patch.

Brer Fox watched and waited. He was listening for Brer Rabbit's cries. Instead he heard *lippety-clippety, clippety-lippety*.

"Ha, ha, ha!" sang Brer Rabbit. "Hee, hee, hee! I was born in the briar patch, Brer Fox. It can't hurt me. I know my way around it like the back of my paw."

And full of glee at his trickery, Brer Rabbit skipped his way home.

The Inch Prince

Mr. and Mrs. Sato lived in a little house in the Japanese countryside.

They had a garden full of healthy plants, and a field full of contented animals. Only one thing could have made them any happier.

"I wish we had a son or a daughter to share our home with," sighed Mrs. Sato one day.

"So do I," said Mr. Sato. "But our house is too small for three people."

"I wouldn't mind a child just one inch tall," suggested his wife.

"That's only as big as my thumb!" laughed Mr. Sato. "No one is that tiny."

At that moment, a wood sprite fluttered by the Satos' window and heard them talking.

She saw the healthy plants and the happy animals. "This couple is kind," she thought. "So I'll be kind to them." She waved her wand over the house and whispered a magic spell.

Not long after, Mr. and Mrs. Sato had a little baby boy... and he was just one inch tall.

They named him Issun-boshi, or Issy for short.

As the years passed, the Satos' plants grew bigger, and their animals grew fatter. But Issy never got any taller. No one seemed to mind.

One day, Issy decided to look for a job in the big city. Carrying a tiny needle for a sword, in case he met monsters, Issy set off.

After a long journey, he
arrived at the Emperor's
palace and strode up
to the gate.
"I've come to see the
Emperor for a job," Issy
announced to the guards,
with a confident air.
The guards laughed.
"What can *you* do?"

"I can run past you, for a start," said Issy.
And he raced into the courtyard, where a
maid was washing the royal socks.

"I've come for a job," said Issy, firmly.
The maid laughed. "What can *you* do?"

"I can run past you, for a start," said Issy.
And he dashed into the kitchen, where the
cook was preparing the royal dinner.

"I've come for a job," said Issy, boldly.
The cook laughed. "What can *you* do?"

"I can run past you, for a start," said Issy. And he sprinted into the throne room where the Emperor was addressing his court.

Issy bowed politely. "I'd like a job please, your Majesty," he said.

"Would you, indeed?" smiled the Emperor.

"But he's tiny, Daddy," said Princess Mizuki. "What can *he* do?"

"Well, I ran past your guards, your maid and your cook to get here," said Issy.

"In that case, I'll make you the princess's bodyguard," declared the Emperor, with a grin.

From then on, Issy never left the princess's side.

One day, they were walking through a forest when a horrible ogre jumped out.

"Ah, lunchtime!" he said, grabbing Mizuki.

"Put her down!" cried Issy.

The ogre laughed. "What can *you* do?" he said, and he popped Issy in his mouth.

Issy whipped out his sword and pricked the ogre's tongue.

"Owwww!" yelled the ogre. He spat Issy out and ran off in pain.

"Thanks, Issy," said Princess Mizuki. "Hey look, the ogre left his hammer behind." She bent to pick it up, but it was too heavy. "I wish you were bigger, Issy," she said. "Then maybe you could lift it."

In a flash, Issy was as tall as the princess.

"The hammer must be magic," said Issy. "It granted your wish."

She smiled. Even before his transformation, Mizuki had begun to fall in love with Issy, and soon she agreed to marry him. For whether he was short or tall, he was always brave.

The Wild Swans

Far away and long ago, there was a land where the swallows flew to spend the winter. The King of that land had lost his wife but she had left him eleven sons and a daughter, Elisa. For a while they lived happily in the palace, but then the King married again.

His new wife hated children and decided at once to be rid of them. She sent Elisa away to live with peasants until her fifteenth birthday.

To the poor princes, she said, "Fly out into the world. Fly away like big birds without a voice."

They turned into eleven magnificent wild swans and flew away, out of the palace window and over the woods beyond.

They tried to stop by the peasant hut
where Elisa lived, craning their long necks and
flapping their wings. But they felt themselves
forced to fly on, high up near the clouds
and away, into the wide, wide world.

They came down in a dark forest that
stretched to the shores of the sea.

Elisa stayed in the peasant
hut, longing for the day
when she turned
fifteen and was at
last allowed home.

But when the
Queen saw how
beautiful she had
become, she was filled with spite.
She smeared Elisa's face with dirt and rubbed
mud into her hair. Elisa was brought before
the King, who looked at his daughter blankly,
no longer recognizing her.

In despair, Elisa ran away to the woods.

She washed herself in a deep clear pool, then wandered on, never knowing where she was going, wishing that, somehow, she could find her brothers.

She followed a river where it flowed into the great open sea and sat down to watch the waves. At sunset, she saw eleven white swans, with golden crowns on their heads, flying towards the shore. As they flew, one behind the other, they looked like a white ribbon floating in the air.

As soon as the sun went down beyond the sea, the swans threw off their feathers and there stood eleven handsome princes.

"My brothers!" cried Elisa, calling out their names. They knew her at once.

"We live on a land across the sea," they told her. "It is only at night that we become human. And we are allowed back to our homeland just once a year. Tomorrow we must fly away once more."

"Take me with you," pleaded Elisa. When they agreed, she at last lay down to rest.

As morning broke, Elisa was woken by the rustling of swans' wings overhead. She opened her eyes and saw that she was in a net of willow bark, being carried across the sky.

All day, her brothers flew like arrows whipping through the air, but as the sun sank down they were forced to take refuge on a jagged black rock. They clung to each other as the waves beat against them, and Elisa had only one thought as she drifted to sleep.

"Please, let me dream how to set my brothers free."

In her dream, she flew to a palace in the clouds and a fairy, shining and fair, flew out to meet her.

"If you are brave," she said, "you can set your brothers free. You must make each one a shirt out of nettles. When they put them on, the spell will be broken. But you must remain silent until the last shirt is finished. Speak just one word, and your brothers die."

She touched Elisa's hand with nettles. They stung her like fire and she woke.

The swans flew again all day, carrying Elisa, until they reached the mountainous land where the brothers now lived.

They set her down beside a cave that was surrounded with nettles. At once she began to weave, though the nettles stung and blistered her hands. Her brothers looked on, hating to see her in pain, but understanding her task.

She worked alone every day, until a hunting party, led by the King of the land, happened to pass her cave.

When the King saw Elisa he fell in love, and took her back with him to his palace. Elisa begged with her eyes to be allowed to stay in her cave, but she could not say a word.

She spent every day weaving her nettles, even as the King planned their marriage. But then, the night before her wedding, she used her last nettle.

"I must find more," she thought. "I still have one last shirt to make."

She tiptoed out into the moonlight,
down to a graveyard where she'd seen nettles
grow. One of the King's advisers saw her go.

"She's a witch!"
he cried. "Seize her!"
he ordered the
palace guards.
"She must have put
a spell on the King."

Elisa was thrown
into prison.

"We'll execute her
tomorrow," said the King's men. The King
was in tears, but there was nothing he could
do to save her.

That night, as she lay in her dungeon, the
guards gave her a pillow of nettles and for a
cover, threw her the nettle shirts. Elisa was
never more glad. She had time to make a
final shirt.

Before day broke, she saw a swan at her window. It was her youngest brother. He gazed at her before tearing himself away.

Elisa rode in a cart to her execution, weighed down by chains but desperately trying to finish the shirt.

"Witch! Witch!" the people jeered as she went by.

Then eleven swans flew down and formed a protective ring around her, flapping their strong, white wings.

"Is it a sign?" the people whispered. "Is she innocent?"

As the executioner seized her, Elisa threw the shirts over the swans. In an instant they were transformed into princes. Only the youngest brother still had one wing, where a sleeve was missing from the last shirt.

"Now I can speak," cried Elisa. "I am innocent."

As she spoke her chains turned to white roses, petals fluttering to the ground. The King picked a flower and gave it to Elisa. "Will you still marry me?" he asked.

"I will," smiled Elisa.

Elisa, the King and her brothers returned to the palace in triumph, and joyfully celebrated the wedding.

The Fisherman and his Wife

O nce upon a time, a fisherman and his wife lived in a tumbledown shack by the sea. Every day, the fisherman went out in his boat, casting his line out to sea, until one incredible day, he caught a fish that could talk.

"Don't eat me," begged the fish, "for I am an enchanted prince."

The fisherman gasped and unhooked the fish as gently as he could. Not knowing what to do next, he put the fish in a jar...

...and carried it back home to his wife.

"No catch today, then?" grumbled his wife.

"Just this," said the fisherman, putting the jar on the table. "It's a *talking* fish."

"Well I never!" said his wife. Her eyes narrowed. "A magic fish, eh? Can you grant me a wish?"

"Anything you like," replied the fish.

The fisherman's wife rubbed her hands with glee. "I'll have a fine house then," she said, "beautiful clothes and plenty of gold."

"Done," said the fish. And it was. The fisherman and his wife danced for joy.

"I want MORE!" declared the
fisherman's wife.

"Isn't this enough?" asked the fisherman.

"No!" said his wife. She looked at the fish.

"Make me richer!" she cried.

"Done," said the fish. And it was.

Their house turned into a palace. Their
boat turned into a yacht. Their clothes were
suddenly threaded with gold and dripping
with jewels.

"Ha, ha!" cried the fisherman's wife.

"This is more than I have ever dreamed of," said the fisherman.

"Not I," said his wife. "Come on, little fishy... I want to be royal! Make us King and Queen."

The fish shook his head and sighed. "Too greedy," he said.

The gold and jewels disappeared. The fine clothes turned back to rags. The palace turned back into a shack... and the fisherman and his wife are still sitting there, in disbelief, today.

The Monkey King

Long ago, in China, there was a monkey who was very, very clever – and very, very naughty. He called himself the Monkey King, and he was always stealing things and starting fights. He caused so much trouble that the Emperor of Heaven wanted to keep an eye on him. So he offered Monkey a job in Heaven.

"I am the great Monkey King," sniffed Monkey. "What position will you give me?"

"Well," sighed the Emperor. "You could be Keeper of the Heavenly Peach Garden."

"Mmmm, peaches..." said Monkey, licking his lips. "I accept!"

An under-gardener showed Monkey the garden. "These are magic peaches," he said. "The orange peaches make you fly, and the yellow ones make you wise..."

"I'm clever enough already," drawled Monkey, with a snigger.

"But the purple peaches are the most precious," the gardener went on. "They take nine thousand years to ripen, and eating one will make you live forever."

"Amazing!" cried Monkey.

Not long after Monkey had begun his new job, he spotted a ripe purple peach among the leaves. "I wonder what it tastes like?" he thought, and gobbled it up.

It was so
delicious, he did
the same thing the
next time he found a ripe
purple peach... and the next...
and the next...

Eventually, the time came for the
Emperor's annual Peach Banquet. Servants
arrived laden with baskets to pick the peaches.
They found plenty of yellow and orange fruit,
but where the purple peaches should have
been, there were only broken branches and
torn leaves.

"Where's that Monkey?" they cried. "The
Emperor will be furious!"

Monkey was sitting in a tree listening.
"Uh-oh," he thought. "Time to get out of
here." And he ran away to Earth.

The Emperor sent soldiers to bring
Monkey back to Heaven. But Monkey had

eaten so many purple peaches, he had become incredibly strong and impossible to harm. The soldiers couldn't make him move an inch.

In despair, the Emperor sent Buddha – the most powerful lord in Heaven.

"You must behave better," Buddha told Monkey sternly.

"Why should I listen to you?" snapped Monkey. "I am the great Monkey King! I am so strong, I will live forever. *I* should be the Emperor of Heaven."

Buddha laughed and held up his hand. "Can you leap beyond my hand?" he asked. "If you do, I will make you Emperor. If you fail, you must accept your punishment."

"Easy," scoffed Monkey, turning to spring into the air.

He whizzed through the clouds... and landed beside five tall, pink pillars.

"The pillars at the end of the world," he chuckled.

"I've won!" He scrawled his name on one pillar, and rudely relieved himself on another, before leaping back into the air...

When he returned, Buddha hadn't moved.

"Silly Monkey," he said. "You didn't leave my hand the whole time."

"Nonsense," scoffed Monkey. "I got to the end of the world, and wrote my name on a pillar to prove it!"

Buddha shook his head. "Just look at my hand."

Monkey looked. There, on one finger, was a familiar scrawl – and there was a funny smell too. He gulped. The pillars *had* looked like giant fingers... "Time to go," he thought.

Before he could move, Buddha lifted his hand. Rocks rained down, trapping Monkey in a stony mountain prison.

"And there you will stay," Buddha told him, "until you are ready to change your ways."

Sleeping Beauty

Once upon a time, a King and Queen had a beautiful baby daughter. One thousand guests were invited to the baby's christening and seven fairies were asked to be godmothers. Each fairy in turn fluttered forward, blessing her with gifts of beauty, cleverness, grace, joy, health, happiness…

"YOU DIDN'T INVITE ME?" thundered a terrible voice. It was the oldest fairy in the kingdom. She hadn't been seen for fifty years and everyone had forgotten her.

"My gift is death," she spat. "When the princess is sixteen she will prick her finger on a spinning wheel and die."

As the King and Queen sobbed, another fairy comforted them.

"I haven't yet given the baby my gift. Alas, I can only soften, not banish, the spell. The princess won't die. She will sleep for a hundred years until a prince wakes her with a kiss."

The very next day, the King ordered that every spinning wheel and spindle in his kingdom be destroyed.

The princess grew up to be as charming as she was beautiful. One day, shortly after her sixteenth birthday, she was exploring the castle and found a tower she had never seen before. At the top of the stairs, she discovered a tiny room where an old lady sat spinning.

"That looks fun!" exclaimed the princess. "May I try?"

"Of course," said the old lady, but no sooner had the princess bent to the spinning wheel than she pricked her finger and fell sound asleep.

Her horrified parents found her and shook her, but she didn't stir. Distraught, they ordered the servants to lay her on her bed. And then they yawned.

The fairy's spell was a powerful one. Everybody in the castle fell asleep: the King and Queen in the throne room; the prime minister in his office; dukes and earls, footmen, maids and cooks; soldiers, horses, grooms and gardeners. Even the princess's little dog lay down, curled up and snored.

Gradually, wild roses sprang up and thorns and bushes grew all over the castle, till every tower and battlement was hidden from view.

One day, a hundred years later, a prince rode by and asked what lay behind this tangled heap of twisting branches.

"Nobody knows," his servants said. "An ogre? Ghosts? Maybe a wizard... Best leave it alone, sire."

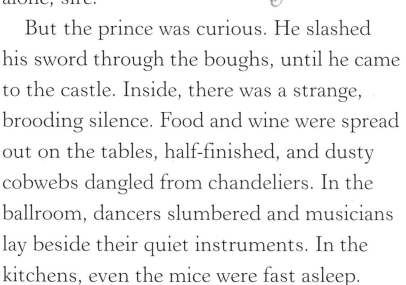

But the prince was curious. He slashed his sword through the boughs, until he came to the castle. Inside, there was a strange, brooding silence. Food and wine were spread out on the tables, half-finished, and dusty cobwebs dangled from chandeliers. In the ballroom, dancers slumbered and musicians lay beside their quiet instruments. In the kitchens, even the mice were fast asleep.

Bewildered, the prince went upstairs. There he found the princess in her bedroom.

She looked so beautiful, as she lay in bed with closed eyes, that he kissed her.

Instantly, the princess awoke. At this first glance, they fell in love. As the princess's little dog barked and wagged his tail, the princess agreed to marry the prince.

By the time they reached the throne room, everyone in the castle was awake. The prince and princess were married at once and, since no one needed to sleep for a while, the celebrations lasted a month.

Hansel and Gretel

Hansel and Gretel lived near a great forest with their father, a poor woodcutter, and their stepmother. One night the children, unable to sleep for hunger, heard her say, "We have no food, husband. We cannot take care of the children any more. Tomorrow, we must leave them in the forest."

"Never!" cried their father, imagining his children torn to pieces by wild animals, but his wife gave him no peace until he agreed.

"Someone will find them and take them in," she reassured him. "And they will only starve if they stay with us."

Gretel looked at Hansel in horror.

"Don't worry," he whispered. Quietly, he slipped outside and collected a pocketful of white pebbles.

He was back in bed before anyone noticed.

"We're going to the forest to chop wood," announced their stepmother, the next day. "You children can gather sticks for the fire."

Every now and then along the way, Hansel dropped a pebble on the path. When night fell, and the children found themselves alone in the dark, shadowy forest, the line of pebbles shone in the moonlight and led them home. Their father was delighted; their stepmother furious.

"We'll try again," she hissed.

"I'd rather share my last crust with them..." he began, but again, he was overruled.

This time Hansel snatched a piece of bread
and secretly crumbled it along the forest path.

That evening, when the children tried
to go home, they found their line
of crumbs had vanished.
Woodland birds had eaten
every morsel and the
pair were well and
truly lost.

Deeper and deeper into the forest they
roamed, hungry, tired and frightened. After
wandering for hours, they came to a house –
the most incredible house they had ever seen,
for it was made entirely of gingerbread and
decorated with sugar paste and marzipan.

Unable to help himself, Hansel broke off
a chunk of the window ledge, just as an old
woman opened the door.

"Dear children, you must be starving if you're eating my house." She grinned. "Why not stay with me? You can eat all you want."

What a fine feast I'll have, she thought to herself, for she was a witch and thought little children a tasty treat.

She cooked them a wonderful supper and Hansel and Gretel went to bed feeling full for the first time in months. But the very next morning, when they came downstairs, the witch grabbed Hansel and shoved him in a shed. "Your breakfast's in there," she said.

"What are you doing?" he shouted.

"Fattening you for my cooking pot," she snarled, locking the door. She turned to Gretel. "And don't stand there blubbing, girl. There's work to do."

For the next few days, she made Gretel wash dishes and scrub floors, while Hansel was fed delicious food through a small hole at the bottom of the shed.

Every morning, the witch barked, "Put out your finger, so I can feel how fat you've grown."

Hansel always stuck out a twig instead, so that the witch, who had weak eyes, wondered why he was still thin.

Four weeks later, when he seemed not the least bit bigger, she screamed, "Whether Hansel be fat or lean, I'm eating him NOW! Open the oven, Gretel and creep in to see if it's hot enough."

Gretel thought quickly. "I'll never fit in there," she said. "No one could."

"Even I could fit, you silly girl," snapped the witch. "Watch!" and she put her own head in the oven.

At once, Gretel pushed her right in and slammed the door. How the witch howled! Gretel ran to set Hansel free.

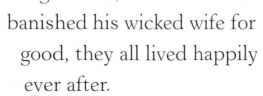

When they explored the witch's house, they found a treasure chest, heaped with glittering jewels. Filling a bag with rubies, emeralds and sapphires, they set off through the forest to try and find home.

By dusk, they reached their father's house. He could hardly believe they had come back. He kissed them and hugged them, then kissed them again and, as he had now banished his wicked wife for good, they all lived happily ever after.

The Lion and the Mouse

One hot, sleepy afternoon, a little mouse was scurrying through the forest. He was in such a hurry to reach his cool, dark mousehole, he didn't hear the rumbling snores, or see the toothy jaws ahead... and *bump!* He ran straight into a sleeping lion.

"How dare you disturb me?" growled the lion, enraged to be woken. He fixed the mouse with a threatening eye. "I should eat you up!"

"I'm s-s-sorry," squeaked the mouse. "If you let me go, I promise I'll repay your kindness."

"Ha, ha," roared the lion. "How could a tiny mouse help me, the King of the Beasts? You've given me such a good laugh, I feel like being kind. Run along now, before I change my mind."

The little mouse didn't hesitate. Off he scampered, and never looked back.

A few months later, he was in the forest when he heard an angry, muffled, "R-r-r-roar!"

"The lion," he thought. "And it sounds like he's in trouble."

He was right. The lion had fallen into a trap and was helplessly tangled in a thick net of ropes. Nimbly, the mouse climbed up and sank his teeth into the ropes. He nibbled and gnawed... until *snap!* The lion tumbled free.

"Thank you," sighed the lion, smiling down at the little mouse. "You saved me! I was wrong to laugh at you. I see now even little friends can be a great big help."

The Princess and the Pea

There was once a prince who longed to marry a real princess. But try as he might, he couldn't find one. And so he lived a sad and lonely life, with only his mother, the Queen, for company.

One wild, wet evening, a stranger turned up at their palace, the rain streaming from her hair. "Please may I sleep here tonight?" she asked. "This storm is very bad and I'm a long way from home."

"Of course," said the prince.

The stranger smiled, a tiara glinting in her rain-wet hair.

"You're a princess?" said the prince, hopefully.

The stranger nodded.

The prince and princess spent the evening talking and laughing together, and by nightfall they were in love.

"She certainly *seems* like a real princess," thought the Queen, watching, "but how to make sure?" Then, she had an idea. "I'll make up a bed for our guest myself," she told the startled housekeeper. "Just find me a pea..."

The Queen slipped the pea under a sheet. On top, she piled twenty soft, puffy mattresses, with twenty soft, fluffy eiderdowns. "Only a *real* princess would be sensitive enough to feel a pea through all that," she thought.

The pile was so high, the princess had to go to bed with a ladder. She thought it a peculiar arrangement, but she was too polite to say so.

In the morning, she came down to breakfast with tired eyes.

"How did you sleep?" asked the Queen.

The princess hesitated. "It was very strange," she admitted, "but I couldn't get comfortable. There was such a lump in the mattress..."

The prince laughed. "I *knew* you were a real princess!" he said. "Hurrah! Will you marry me?"

"Oh yes," agreed the princess, smiling.

And so they were married, and the pea was put in the palace museum as a memento. And, if you visit, you may see it there still.

The Royal
Pea

Tiddalik

Long, long ago, in the Dreamtime, when the world was first beginning, lived the largest frog there ever was. His name was Tiddalik. One morning, he woke with a terrible thirst. "I need a drink," he declared.

He slurped up water from the frothy springs. He gurgled and guzzled the burbling streams. He drank every last drop of the billabongs and bogs, and drained the rivers and lakes.

But he was STILL thirsty. So he began to search for rain clouds, with great flicks from his long slimy tongue.

Catching the clouds with his tongue, he
pulled them from the sky, then burst them
inside his mouth so a million raindrops
dripped down his throat.

His body swelled, grew round and huge.
He had finally quenched his thirst.

But without water, the world withered. The
ground cracked. Plants wilted, turned yellow
and died. Leaves dropped from the trees and
the trees dropped to the ground, until the
ground itself heaved a sigh and whimpered,
"Help, I am dying of thirst."

The animals realized that something had
to be done. They came together by the
dried-up banks of the Molonglo River, to see
if they could save the world.

"Tiddalik must give us back our water," snapped the crocodile.

"But how?" squawked the parrots.

"We must make Tiddalik laugh," said the wise old wombat. "If we can get him to open his mouth, the water will come gushing out."

So the animals rushed to find him, down on the Kwongan Sands. The kookaburra kicked off with his very best joke. The emu laughed so loud that the wattled bats woke. But Tiddalik took no notice.

The kangaroos jumped through hoops, while the blue-tongued skink turned her tongue pink.

"What a hoot!" laughed the rabbit-eared bandicoot.

But Tiddalik took no notice. For days the animals joked and danced,

without a flicker of interest from the swollen
frog. Then, at last, the eel slithered onto
the scene.

He twirled around, he jumped up and
down, and for the first time, Tiddalik
forgot to frown.

The eel leaped up again and wobbled his
body. Tiddalik's smile spread over his face and
his bulging cheeks began to shake.

For his final act, the eel stood on one spot,
then tied his body in a series of knots. Tiddalik
clutched his stomach and let out a loud
guffaw. The water gushed out from his gaping
mouth with a deafening, thunderous roar.

The water seeped into the cracks in the dried-up ground, then bubbled back up in the springs. It poured from there into babbling brooks, which flowed into rivers, which fed the lakes, until the world was awash with water once more.

The sky grew darker, the clouds grew bigger, until one by one they burst. Then down it came, great buckets of rain, bringing life back to the land at last.

Tiddalik looked on in shame. "I promise," he croaked, "never to be so greedy again."

The Magic Melon

Lee lived in a little village surrounded by steep green rice fields. All summer long, the villagers worked hard in the fields, while Lee lazed in the sunshine. He snored while they planted the rice. He snoozed while they harvested it.

At last, the smell of fresh-cooked rice filled the air..."Dinner time," yawned Lee.

But the villagers didn't want to share. "You're just a lazy bones!" they scolded. "If you didn't help grow the rice, you can't help eat it."

Lee's tummy rumbled. "What shall I do?" he wondered. He looked around – and noticed an old man with a melon. "I'm so hungry," he moaned. "Please may I have some melon?"

"No," said the man. Lee's face fell. "This is a magic melon," the man explained, more kindly. "What do you really want to eat?"

"Fried rice," sighed Lee, licking his lips.

The man tapped the melon and – *ping!* There was a bowl of sizzling hot fried rice.

"Amazing," gasped Lee, as he gobbled up the rice. "I wish *I* had a magic melon."

"You can grow one," said the man. "But it's not easy." He held out a tiny seed. "You must dig the ground carefully when you plant it, and then water it three times a day."

"I will," promised Lee. And to begin with, he did. But it was hard work and he was soon bored. "I'll just have a quick snooze," he thought...

Every day, Lee snoozed, while the melon grew... When at last it was round and ripe, he picked it.

"Mmm, fried rice," he said happily. He tapped the melon and – *ping!* There was a dry crust of bread. "W-w-what?" he stammered.

Behind him, someone laughed. It was the old man. "You didn't take care of the melon," he said, as Lee hung his head. "You cheated it – so now it's cheating you!"

The Three Little Pigs

There were once three little pigs who lived with their mother. But they grew and grew, as little pigs do, until they grew too big for their mother's house. So they went out into the world to find homes of their own.

They trotted along happily, until they met a man selling bundles of straw.

"Look," squeaked the first pig. "I'm going to build a straw cottage." And he did.

The other pigs trotted on, until they met a man selling sticks.

"Look," grunted the
second pig. "I'm going
to build a wood cabin."
And he did.

"Straw and sticks are all
very well," snorted the third pig.
"But I want something stronger." So she
walked on, until she met a man selling bricks.

"Hurrah!" she shouted. "I'm going to build
a house of bricks. Bricks are much stronger
than straw. They're stronger than sticks too...
but gosh, they're *hard work*!"

It took a long time, but at last her house
was finished. She crept inside and
fell asleep.

The very next day, a big,
bad wolf was passing the
straw house when he saw
the first pig inside. "Mmm,
breakfast..." he thought.

He rapped on the door and called out,
"Little pig, little pig, let me come in!"

But the pig had seen who it was. "Not by
the hair on my chinny-chin-chin," he cried.

"Then I'll huff and I'll puff, and I'll
BLOW your house in!" growled
the wolf. He took a deep
breath. *Huff!* The straw
walls wobbled.
Puff! They blew
completely away.

The first pig squealed and ran to his
brother's house, with the wolf hot on
his heels.

"Little pigs, little pigs, let me come in!"

"Not by the hair on our chinny-chin-chins."

"Then I'll huff and I'll puff, and I'll BLOW
your house in!" snarled the wolf.

Huff! The wood creaked. *Puff!* It cracked.
Huff! It split into splinters. The two pigs

squealed and raced to their sister's house. The wolf was right behind them.

"Little pigs, little pigs, let me come in!"

"Not by the hair on our chinny-chin-chins."

"Then I'll huff and I'll puff, and I'll BLOW your house in!" howled the wolf. *Huff! Puff! Huff! Puff!* Nothing. The bricks were simply too strong.

The wolf refused to give up. In two bounds, he leaped onto the roof and shot down the chimney... *Splosh!* He had landed in the cooking pot. The little pigs slammed on the lid – and that was the end of him.

As for the three pigs, they lived together in the strong brick house, happily ever after.

The Ant and the Grasshopper

All summer, the Grasshopper chirruped among the flowers, dancing from blossom to blossom. He was green, long-limbed and beautiful. Bright as an emerald, his body glittered as he leaped in the sunshine, and his voice soared in a song of glorious music. Scurrying in the undergrowth, the Ant was busy. He was gathering wheat to store for wintertime when food would be scarce, and all the animals of the woodland and heath would be hungry.

"Work or starve," said the Ant to himself. "It's as simple as that."

He had to pluck each ear of wheat and every seed, and carry them, one by one, to his larders, again and again, hundreds of times, to fill his cellar. He was tired, working so hard in the heat, but he never gave up. He was thinking of his family. He wanted them to survive the winter.

When winter clutched the earth with icy fingers, the Grasshopper didn't feel like singing or dancing any more. He was hungry, but there was nothing to eat. The ground was hard, the trees were bare, the grass was withered, the flowers were dead. Summer was forgotten under a blanket of unforgiving snow.

The Grasshopper came across the Ant – such a plump, happy, well-fed-looking creature.

"Please," begged the Grasshopper, "have you any food to spare for me? I have nothing."

"Why not?" asked the Ant. "What were you doing all summer?"

"I sang," said the Grasshopper. "I danced."

"You sang? You danced? Very well," sneered the Ant, turning away. "Play on."

"Why won't you help me?"

"I worked, while you enjoyed yourself. You were lazy and thoughtless. Why should you benefit from my toil?"

"But I'll starve to death," wept the Grasshopper.

The Ant took pity on him and gave him some corn. "Just remember, there's a time to work and a time to play," he said. "Perhaps next summer you'll think about the winter ahead."

"Oh I will," promised the Grasshopper.

Midas and the Golden Touch

King Midas was a kind man. He was also a wealthy one, but all the gold in his palace didn't keep him from dreaming of more.

One day, Midas was out walking when he met an elderly man. The man looked so tired that Midas invited him to the palace to rest.

Within minutes, a worried young man appeared. He wore a leafy crown and his skin had a strange glow. "There you are!" he exclaimed, dashing up to the man and hugging him. "I've been looking everywhere for you."

The old man smiled and turned to Midas. "This is Dionysus," he said. "He's a god."

Dionysus looked at Midas. "Thank you for taking such good care of my friend," he said. "In return, I will give you a wish."

Midas didn't hesitate. "I wish everything I touched would turn to gold."

Dionysus frowned. "Are you sure? I don't think it's a good idea."

"Oh I'm sure," said Midas eagerly.

"So be it," sighed Dionysus, snapping his fingers... "But don't say I didn't warn you."

Midas felt something heavy in his hands and glanced down. His stick shone bright gold. "Amazing," he gasped. "Thank you!"

Midas picked a rose – and the petals froze into golden curls. A fly buzzed past and he swatted it. A moment later, a solid gold fly hit the ground with a *ching*.

Laughing, Midas touched his palace – and the walls turned to dazzling gold. He blinked and grinned. "I must be the richest man in the world!" he said.

By then, it was dinnertime. Hungrily, Midas picked up his food and took a large bite...

"Ow!" The meat had turned to gleaming metal. Next, he tried to take a drink. "Pfffft!" The water had hardened into golden ice.

"Oh no!" wailed Midas. He got down on his knees to Dionysus. "This is awful. Please make it stop."

The god took pity on the King. "There is a river in the hills," he told him. "It will wash away your gift, if you bathe in it."

It was a long walk, but at last Midas found the river. The water flowed fast and cold. He stepped in nervously, hardly daring to look...

"Hurrah!" His stick was just a wooden stick again. At the same moment, his palace became ordinary stone, his food turned back into food, and a confused fly twitched back to life.

Midas' gift was gone – although people say the sands of the river sparkle with gold to this day.

"Gold is all very well," Midas sighed in relief, "but I'd rather be able to eat!"

Chicken Licken

Once upon a time, there was a tiny chick named Chicken Licken. He was scared of anything and everything – even his own shadow.

One day, he was sitting under a mighty oak tree when he felt something land, *bonk*, on his head.

"Oh my gosh!" he cried. "The sky is falling. I must warn the King." He jumped up and ran back to the farm.

Henny Penny was sitting by the hen house.

"The sky is falling!" yelled Chicken Licken.

"Oh my dear!" said Henny Penny. "Whatever shall we do?"

"I'm going to warn the King," said Chicken Licken. He rushed off, with Henny Penny close behind. They dashed across the farm.

There was Cocky Locky, strutting around.

"The sky is falling!" yelled Chicken Licken.

"Oh my word!" said Cocky Locky. "Whatever shall we do?"

"We're going to warn the King," clucked Henny Penny.

Chicken Licken raced on, with Henny Penny and Cocky Locky close behind. They came to the pond.

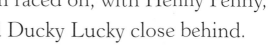

Ducky Lucky was there, swimming around.

"The sky is falling!" yelled Chicken Licken.

"Oh my goodness!" said Ducky Lucky. "Whatever shall we do?"

"We're going to warn the King," squawked Cocky Locky.

Chicken Licken raced on, with Henny Penny, Cocky Locky and Ducky Lucky close behind.

They came to the old barn.

Goosey Loosey was there, building a nest.

"The sky is falling!" yelled Chicken Licken.

"Oh my stars!" said Goosey Loosey. "Whatever shall we do?"

"We're going to warn the King," quacked Ducky Lucky.

Chicken Licken raced on, with Henny Penny, Cocky Locky, Ducky Lucky and Goosey Loosey close behind. They came to the meadow on the edge of the farm.

There was Turkey Lurkey, scratching in the ground for worms.

"The sky is falling!" yelled Chicken Licken.

"Oh my gracious!" said Turkey Lurkey. "Whatever shall we do?"

"We're going to warn the King," honked Goosey Loosey.

Chicken Licken rushed off, with Henny Penny, Cocky Locky, Ducky Lucky, Goosey Loosey and Turkey Lurkey close behind. They came to the woods.

Foxy Loxy was dozing in the shade.

"The sky is falling!" cried Chicken Licken. "We're going to warn the King."

Foxy Loxy didn't believe Chicken Licken, but he didn't say so. "You're in luck. I know a short-cut to the King's palace," he said, pointing to a hole in the ground.

"In you go, quickly!"

The birds ran into the hole. But it wasn't a short-cut to the palace at all. It was Foxy Loxy's den.

"Now I'm going to gobble you up," he cried.

Just then, he felt something land, *bonk*, on his head. It was only an acorn, but Foxy Loxy didn't see it.

"Oh my heavens!" he yelped. "The sky really is falling." And he ran off in fright.

Cocky Locky turned to Chicken Licken. "Are you *sure* the sky fell on your head?" he asked.

Chicken Licken went bright red. "I suppose it *might* have been an acorn," he gulped.

"Chicken Licken!" screeched the birds, and they chased the little chick all the way home.

Aladdin

There was once a boy named Aladdin. After his father died, he and his mother had little money and never enough to eat.

They had almost given up hope, when a stranger knocked on their door.

"Greetings!" he cried. "I'm Aladdin's long-lost uncle, Abanazar. I've been away and only just heard the news of my poor brother. I've come to set up Aladdin in business."

Aladdin and his mother were so relieved to hear this, they didn't think to question it, though neither had heard of Abanazar before. In fact, he was a wicked magician who wanted a magic lamp, and had read in his books that only Aladdin could help him.

He took Aladdin to a deserted patch of ground outside the city.

"I have an errand for you," Abanazar announced. He lit a fire, scattering powder as he murmured strange words.

Aladdin couldn't believe his eyes as the

ground shimmered and a trapdoor appeared.

"There's a lamp down there," said Abanazar. "I want you to bring it to me. As a reward, you may have this," and he handed Aladdin a ring topped with a gleaming ruby.

"Certainly, Uncle!" Aladdin said.

He climbed down into a cave. It was dark and smelly, and Aladdin didn't like it much,

but he crept further in and soon found the
lamp. As his eyes grew used to the gloom,
he saw four rooms crammed with gold.
Beyond them was a shining garden of trees,
blossoming with glistening jewels. Quickly, he
grabbed handfuls of treasure, before hurrying
back to the entrance.

The moment he reappeared, Abanazar
bellowed, "Where's my lamp?"

"Please may I come out?" said Aladdin,
who didn't want to stay in the murky cave a
second longer.

"You didn't find it?" Abanazar
yelled, and he slammed the door shut.

Aladdin was terrified. Surely this
cruel man couldn't really be his
uncle? Shivering in the
dark, he rubbed
his hands to
keep warm.

He didn't realize he was also rubbing the ring...

A man loomed out of the darkness and Aladdin jumped back in shock.

"I am the genie of the ring. Your wish is my command."

"I want to go home," wailed Aladdin. In a trice, he found himself magically whisked back to his mother. She was thrilled with the jewels he'd brought but she was not impressed with the lamp.

"Dirty old thing," she said. "I'll sell it, once I've cleaned it up."

As she polished it, an enormous man appeared and announced, "I am the genie of the lamp. Your wish is my command."

"Food, please," Aladdin

ordered, laughing at his astonished mother, who nearly dropped the lamp.

Instantly, a delicious feast was spread before them on solid silver plates. It lasted an entire week, and then Aladdin sold the plates in the market. With the money jingling in his pocket, he went for a stroll and saw the Sultan's beautiful daughter, Badroulbourdour, who was out with her ladies-in-waiting. The two exchanged smiles and Aladdin fell in love.

"I have to marry her," he told his mother.

"But she's a princess!"

"Mother, I love her. Will you take the jewels I found to the Sultan, as a gift?"

Aladdin's mother hated to see him unhappy, so she showed the Sultan the jewels.

"These are from my son who wishes to marry Princess Badroulbourdour," she said.

The Sultan was thrilled. "Lovely! If he can produce forty trays of gold carried by eighty servants dressed in silk and jewels, Badroulbourdour is his."

Aladdin rubbed his lamp and instantly the genie conjured up a procession of glittering treasure and servants marching to the palace.

Aladdin and Badroulbourdour were married and lived happily in a magnificent palace built with the magic of the lamp.

News of the wedding and Aladdin's wealth reached Abanazar, who plotted his revenge.

One morning, when Aladdin had gone out, Abanazar disguised himself as a merchant and walked up and down outside the palace.

"New lamps for old," he called. "New for old!" Badroulbourdour heard him. "Aladdin has a dirty old oil lamp," she thought, and handed Abanazar her husband's precious lamp.

Crowing with glee, Abanazar summoned the genie and had him magic the palace to a distant desert, with the princess still inside it. There Badroulbourdour was trapped, lonely and miserable with only Abanazar for company. She longed for Aladdin.

Aladdin was longing for her too. He had come home to find his wife and palace missing and was devastated. When he heard about the merchant, he guessed what must have happened.

At once, he summoned the genie of the ring.

"Take me to Badroulbourdour!" Aladdin commanded.

As he fell into his wife's arms, he whispered, "We must be free of Abanazar for good. Before he dines with you tonight, drop poison into his wine."

Badroulbourdour nodded. Secretly, she poured the poison and by morning, Abanazar was dead.

Aladdin grabbed his lamp and flew Badroulbourdour, the palace and himself back home.

In time, Aladdin and Badroulbourdour
had a baby and his mother became a proud
grandmother. Aladdin became the Sultan and
all lived happily ever after.

As for the lamp and the ring, they were put
away in a drawer and forgotten. Who knows –
someone might discover them again. The
genies are waiting...

Little Red Riding Hood

Once upon a time, there was a little girl called Little Red Riding Hood who always wore a bright red cloak, with a bright red hood. She lived with her mother on the edge of some rambling woods.

One morning, her mother said, "Your grandmother's not feeling well. Please would you go and visit her?"

"Of course I will," said Little Red Riding Hood. And she set off through the woods to her grandmother's cottage, carrying a basket of food.

At first, the sun shone and the birds sang, but the deeper she went, the darker the woods became. She never saw the wolf waiting for her on the path.

"And where are you going, little girl?" asked the wolf, rubbing his paws together.

"I'm going to grandmother's cottage, on the other side of the woods," said Little Red Riding Hood.

"How delicious…" thought the wolf. "Her grandmother would make a tasty snack. And then I can eat Little Red Riding Hood too…"

The wolf smiled at Little Red Riding Hood. "Why don't you pick her some flowers?" he suggested. "I see a pretty patch of bluebells, just over there."

"What a lovely idea," said Little Red Riding Hood, and she left the path to pick a large bunch of flowers.

As soon as her back was turned, the wolf raced through the woods and knocked on the grandmother's cottage.

"Who's there?" asked the grandmother.

"Your granddaughter, Little Red Riding Hood," squeaked the wolf.

"I've brought you some food."

"Let yourself in," said the grandmother. The wolf leaped into the room and gobbled up Little Red Riding Hood's grandmother in one gulp.

"Mmm," he said, smacking his lips. "Bony, but not bad."

Then he put on the grandmother's nightcap and climbed into bed, to wait for Little Red Riding Hood. Soon, he heard a knock at the door.

"Come in," said the wolf, as sweetly and softly as he could.

"I'm sorry you're not well. I've brought you some food," said Little Red Riding Hood.

"Lovely," snarled the wolf. "I mean *lovely*," he squeaked. "Come and sit next to me, dear."

Little Red Riding Hood looked at her grandmother, then looked again.

"Oh Grandmother! What big ears you have."

"All the better to hear you with," said the wolf.

"Oh Grandmother! What big eyes you have!" said Little Red Riding Hood, coming closer to the bed.

"All the better to see you with," said the wolf.

Little Red Riding Hood came closer still. "Oh Grandmother!" she said. "What big, hairy hands you have."

"All the better to hug you with," said the wolf.

Little Red Riding Hood was now standing right next to the bed. "But Grandmother!" she cried. "What big, sharp teeth you have."

"All the better to eat you with," snapped the wolf.

He jumped out of bed and gobbled up Little Red Riding Hood. "Full at last," he thought.

Then he lay down on the bed and fell fast asleep. As the wolf slept, he snored... very loudly.

"I've never heard the old lady snoring that loudly before," thought a woodcutter, who was passing by. And he went inside the cottage to look. There, he found the wolf, with a big bulge in his tummy.

"He's eaten the old woman!" cried the woodcutter. "Maybe I can still save her!"

So he picked up some scissors and snipped open the wolf's tummy. *Snip, snip...* he saw a bright red hood. *Snip, snip...* out popped Little Red Riding Hood.

"Keep cutting!" she cried. "Grandmother's still in there."

Snippety-snip went the scissors until Grandmother popped out too.

Snore... Snore... The wolf slept on.

"I have an idea," said Little Red Riding Hood. She ran outside, picked up some stones and put them in the wolf's tummy. Then Grandmother sewed him up.

When the wolf woke up he tried to sneak out of the door, but the stones rattled and clattered inside him.

"Now everyone can hear you coming," said Little Red Riding Hood. "You'll never be able to eat another person."

As for Little Red Riding Hood, she never, ever talked to a wolf again.

Persephone

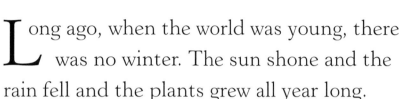

L ong ago, when the world was young, there was no winter. The sun shone and the rain fell and the plants grew all year long.

Demeter, goddess of the harvest, took good care of everything that grew. She lived with her daughter Persephone, whom she loved dearly and protected fiercely.

But Hades, god of the Underworld, had spied Persephone and wanted her for himself.

One afternoon, while she was out with her friends, there was a deafening CRACK!

A huge chasm opened up in the ground beside them and a chariot thundered out.

Before Persephone could say a word, a cloaked figure swept her off her feet and whisked her underground.

When Demeter learned of the capture she rushed to the field, but there was no sign of a chasm and no sign of her daughter.

Over the next year, all Demeter could think of was finding Persephone. She neglected the plants and without her loving touch they withered and died. An endless winter began, and humans and animals were left to starve.

Eventually Demeter's brother Zeus, king of the gods, summoned her to his palace on Mount Olympus.

"Do you have news of Persephone?" she asked anxiously.

"She's been with Hades all along," sighed Zeus. "He loves her and is taking care of her."

"With Hades?" she gasped. "In the land of the dead? You mustn't allow it."

"I was afraid you'd say that," her brother muttered. "I'll see what I can do."

Zeus called for his son Hermes, the messenger god, and sent him to the Underworld to negotiate with Hades. Hermes found the King of the Underworld beside his new Queen, in a dark garden that glittered with gemstones. The only living thing was a small, twisted pomegranate tree.

"What do you want?" bellowed Hades.

"Zeus has sent me," Hermes replied, "to ask after Persephone."

"I am well, thank you," she said nervously. "Hades is kind and caring, but I do miss the sunshine and the sky... and my dear mother."

"Then you shall return with me," said Hermes bravely.

"Never," Hades snorted. "I need her here."

"But Zeus says the world above needs her

too," said Hermes. "All living things are dying because of Demeter's grief. Only Persephone can bring them to life again."

Hades sat in thoughtful silence. Ultimately, he had to obey Zeus, but Zeus had to obey the ancient laws…

"Persephone cannot leave," he announced with sudden triumph. "It's impossible to leave the Underworld if you have eaten while you are here."

"But I only ate six pomegranate seeds!" Persephone protested.

"Exactly," Hades nodded.

Persephone turned pleadingly to Hermes.

"I know," suggested Hermes at last. "For six months of the year, one for every seed you ate, you will stay here with Hades. For the other six months, you will return to Demeter."

Both Hades and Persephone looked pleased with this solution.

When Demeter saw her daughter again, she was overjoyed. Thousands of green shoots sprang through the soil, new leaves unfurled in every tree, and flowers the world over burst into bloom.

As the six months came to an end, so did the summer. Persephone made her way back to Hades in the Underworld and nature joined Demeter in her mourning. But from that time onwards, winter was bearable, because there was always the promise of spring and Persephone's return.

Clever Kallie

Kallie and Kaspar were brother and sister, but as different as they could be. For while Kallie was generous and loving, Kaspar was selfish and proud.

When their aunt gave them a little brown horse to share, Kaspar was furious. "I'm the oldest; it should be mine," he insisted. And he argued and argued, until at last the argument reached the ears of the King.

"We will settle this with riddles," the King told them. "Whoever gives the best answers will keep the horse."

Kaspar grinned. "I'm so clever, this will be easy," he told himself.

"First," said the King, "what is the fastest thing in the world?"

"A racehorse," said Kaspar quickly.

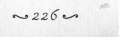

"But the wind is faster," added Kallie. "No horse can outrun the wind."

"What is the heaviest thing in the world?"

"Iron," said Kaspar.

"But the ground is heavier," said Kallie. "It's so heavy, no one can pick it up."

The King laughed. "Finally, what is the most precious thing in the world?"

"Gold," snorted Kaspar.

"Love," said Kallie softly. "People can live happily without gold, but not without love."

The King smiled at her. "The horse is yours," he said. "Well done! I only wish all my people were as clever as Kallie."

Stone Soup

There was once a desperately poor man. All he had in the world was his dog and a shiny stone. He would travel from village to town, looking for work and shelter.

The last few weeks had been hard, with no work anywhere. Luckily it was summer, so he didn't mind sleeping outside, watching the stars in the night sky and listening to the owls hunt. Still, he was getting tired of living on nuts and berries, so when he came across a well-kept cottage, he was delighted.

With his dog at his heels, he strode up the path and knocked on the door.

"Go away!" came a voice from inside.

"Oh dear," thought the man, but he knocked again. This time, the door was opened by a grumpy-looking woman.

"What do you want?" she snapped, glaring at him.

"I wondered if you had any odd jobs I might do?" he asked.

"No," she said.

"Well, could I rest here a while?" he asked. "And maybe we could share lunch?"

"I don't have enough for two," she said. "What have you got?"

The man took the stone from his pocket and held it out.

The woman looked at it disbelievingly.

"That's all you have?" she said. "A stone? You're wasting my time," and she started to close the door.

"Wait!" said the man. "I can make soup from this stone."

"Really?" said the woman. "That I would like to see. I suppose you'd better come in."

"We'll need a large pot of water," said the man, so the woman filled her cauldron and set it on the fire.

"What next?" she asked.

The man dropped in his stone.

"We let it simmer for a while," he said.

The soup began to simmer. The man took a spoon and tasted a mouthful.

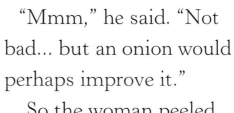

"Mmm," he said. "Not bad... but an onion would perhaps improve it."

So the woman peeled and chopped an onion, and popped it in.

The man stirred the soup and let it simmer some more.

Then he tasted it again.

"Mmm," he said. "Delicious, although a couple of potatoes would make it even better."

"Two potatoes..." said the woman, peeling and chopping them, and dropping them in.

By now, the soup was bubbling away. The man tried a third spoonful.

"Mmm," he said, licking his lips. "Some meat would make it perfect."

"I have some sausage," suggested the woman, slicing it.

She added it to the pot and the man gave the soup another stir.

A wonderful smell filled the cottage. The woman smiled.

The man took a final taste. "Almost there," he said. "We just need a few fresh herbs, and some salt and pepper."

The woman chopped some herbs and sprinkled them in, along with plenty of pepper and salt.

"Done!" said the man. He ladled the soup into bowls and they sat down to eat.

"This soup is scrumptious!" said the woman. "Your stone must be magic."

The man smiled. He washed and dried the stone and put it back in his pocket.

"Would you like to stay for supper?" the woman asked. "We can have more soup!"

The Princess and the Pig Boy

Once, there was a poor prince who wanted to get married, but he didn't want to marry any old princess. He wanted to marry the Emperor's daughter.

"Why shouldn't I?" he thought. "I am a prince, and my father's kingdom, though small, is still a kingdom..."

The prince sent the princess his two finest possessions: a rose tree that produced a single, most magnificent flower, and a nightingale that sang like an angel.

The princess frowned. "Ugh!" she said. "An ugly tree and a boring bird? Send them back."

The prince didn't give up.

He rubbed mud on his face, put on some old clothes, went to the palace and asked for a job. After a brief interview, he was appointed Pig Boy to His Imperial Highness. It wasn't his dream job, but it did give him another chance to impress the princess.

That evening, he slaved away until he had made a magic rattle. When he whirled it around, it played all the polkas and waltzes that had ever been composed.

The princess heard the rattle. "What's making that beautiful music?" she wondered. "I want it."

She followed the music and found the pig boy. "I'd like that rattle," she said.

"It's yours... for one hundred kisses," replied the prince.

"NEVER!" exclaimed the princess. "Can't you just give it to me?" she asked.

The pig boy prince shook his head. "No kisses, no rattle," he said, and played it again.

The princess sighed and gave in. "I hope no one sees us," she said.

But her father, up on his balcony, *did* see. "My daughter kissing a pig boy?" he roared. "Both of you must leave my palace now! And never return."

The princess looked shocked. "But Daddy..." she wailed. "Oh, why didn't I marry the kind prince who sent the nightingale?" she added.

To the Emperor and his daughter's surprise, the pig boy ran behind the sty and changed his clothes. "You still can!" he said, with a grin.

The Hare
and the Tortoise

Hare was fast, and he loved to run. Every morning, he ran to his job at the post office, and then ran around the village, delivering packages at top speed. At the end of the day, Hare ran back home. To relax, he ran a few times around his garden, and at night, he dreamed about running.

The only thing Hare loved apart from running was talking about running. He loved talking about how good it felt to be the fastest animal in town. Not like poor old Tortoise.

Tortoise was slow, and he loved sitting. Every morning, Tortoise got out of bed and shuffled slowly to his job at the post office.

All day long, he sat at his desk, carefully stamping packages.

At the end of the day, Tortoise inched his way home. To relax, he liked sitting in his armchair, with a pot of tea, nibbling cake by the fire. When he dreamed, he even dreamed that he was in his armchair, with a pot of tea, nibbling cake by the fire.

One afternoon, Tortoise was in the middle of stamping a particularly bumpy package, when Hare burst into the post office shouting, "I've had the most brilliant idea!"

Tortoise sighed, as the package slipped and fell to the floor.

"Now, we all know I'm the best runner in the village," said Hare. "But wouldn't it be fun to have a race? One of you might just be able to beat me," he added, with a chuckle.

"I'll challenge you," Tortoise said slowly.

All the animals in the post office turned around. Hare stared at Tortoise in amazement.

"*You* want to race *me*?" said Hare. "Old tottery Tortoise? But – you might expire! And what about the poor people watching the race? They don't want to have to wait up until midnight to watch you go by!"

Hare clutched his stomach and roared with laughter at his own joke.

"I'd still like to try," said Tortoise firmly.

"Well, that's settled then," said Hare, grinning from ear to ear. "Let's race tomorrow!" And he ran off home, thinking about the victory ahead. He'd never have an easier race in his life. That evening, Tortoise's friends tried to change his mind. They knew that Hare would win the race, and then he'd be more vain than ever. But Tortoise had made up his mind.

The next morning, Hare and Tortoise met in the village square, and Tortoise gazed up at the enormous map of the race. The course was many miles long, further than he had ever even walked before.

He stood quietly at the start line as Hare bounced up and down beside him.

"On your marks, get set, go!" shouted Badger, the umpire. They were off.

Hare sprinted forward, and within moments, he had disappeared in a cloud of dust. Tortoise put one foot in front of the other, and trudged across the start line.

He was walking even more slowly than usual. "Must pace myself," he muttered under his breath. "Mustn't wear myself out."

Meanwhile, Hare sped ahead. Soon, he was miles in front of Tortoise. As he reached the crest of a hill, he stopped for a moment and looked back along the road. He could just see a tiny green speck, hardly moving, in the distance.

"Poor old Tortoise," Hare said to himself. "It will be hours before he catches up."

It was a
beautiful day, and
Hare spied a pleasant
shady spot under a
tree. "There's no point
running in the midday
sun," he thought. "I'll lie
under this tree for a moment
and have a quick nap."

Miles behind, Tortoise plodded on. His
feet were sore and his legs ached, but he was
determined to finish the race. The hours
ticked by... Hare slept. In his dreams, he won
race after race after race.

As the sun set behind the hill, a shadow
fell across Hare's face. He opened his eyes,
yawned and jumped to his feet. "The race!"
he shrieked, suddenly wide awake. "The race!"
Hare dashed off down the road, running as
fast as he could.

He ran through a village, over a hill, and soon, in the distance, he could see the finish line... and a small green speck, hardly moving, close to it. "It can't be!" he thought, and ran faster than he had ever run in his life.

Slowly but surely, Tortoise put one foot over the line, as Hare came dashing in, a split second behind him. A huge roar went up from the crowd.

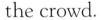

"Tortoise is the champion!" Badger shouted. "Hare, you lost by a whisker."

"Slow and steady wins the race," Tortoise declared.

He had a quiet smile on his face as he shuffled home for a pot of tea and some cake in his armchair by the fire.

Cinderella

Once upon a time, there was a beautiful young girl named Cinderella. She lived with her timid father, her mean stepmother and her two obnoxious stepsisters. Poor Cinderella was constantly bossed around and treated as a servant.

One day, the stepsisters were giddy with excitement. An invitation had arrived for a ball at the royal palace. The prince wanted to choose himself a wife and had invited all the young ladies in the land to attend.

"Fetch our finest dresses, Cinders!" commanded the elder stepsister. "We must look our dazzling best."

"What a shame *maids* aren't invited too," jibed the younger stepsister.

Cinderella dutifully laced up her stepsisters' dresses, styled their hair and helped put on their gaudy jewels, without a word. But once they'd swept off in their coach, she sat down and cried her heart out.

"If only I could go to the ball," she wept.

"Now, now," came a soft voice. "Why so many tears?"

Cinderella turned in surprise to see a little woman with wings. "Wh-who are you?" she stammered. "Wh-what do you want?"

"I'm your fairy godmother and I want you to go to the ball."

Spellbound, Cinderella watched her fairy
godmother whirl around the room. With
a sweep of her wand, she turned a plump
pumpkin into a golden coach, six mice
into proud white horses, a rat into a
handsome coachman and two
lizards into elegant
footmen. Finally,
she transformed
Cinderella's rags into
a sparkling dress with
dainty glass slippers.

"Enjoy yourself," said the fairy,
with a smile, "but be sure you're home by
midnight. That's when my magic wears off."

Cinderella arrived at the ball as if in a
dream. The prince was instantly enchanted
by her and they danced the night away. Only
on the final strike of midnight did Cinderella
realize the time...

Panicked, she fled the palace, losing a slipper in her haste, and arriving home breathless, footsore and in love. The baffled

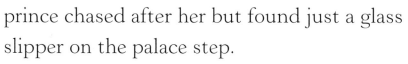

prince chased after her but found just a glass slipper on the palace step.

"Which way did my beautiful princess go?" he asked the guards.

"Princess, sire? We only saw a girl in rags," they replied.

The poor prince toured the kingdom, desperate to find his mysterious princess. He went from house to house, trying the slipper on every woman's foot.

When he reached the stepsisters' house, they snatched the slipper from him and tried in vain to ram it onto their large, lumpy feet.

"May I try?" asked Cinderella.

"Of course not!" scoffed the stepsisters.

"Of course you may," replied the prince.

Amid protests from the stepsisters, Cinderella stepped forward. Her dainty foot was a perfect fit and the prince gasped in delight. With a smile, Cinderella reached into her apron pocket to reveal the matching glass slipper.

The prince and Cinderella were married later that year and everyone in the kingdom was invited to the wedding. Even her two stepsisters came, and were welcomed to the palace from then on, though they didn't grow any less obnoxious.

Icarus, The Boy Who Flew

O n the ancient island of Crete, a father
and son were imprisoned in a tall tower.
The father, Daedalus, was a gifted inventor
and chief designer for King Minos. He'd
invented the first sails, a musical floor to
dance on, even an elaborate maze of tunnels
that could trap a man forever. But when
he helped the King's enemy, Theseus,
to escape from that very maze, he was
sent to prison.

"Why did the King have to lock me
up as well?" complained Daedalus'
son, Icarus.

"Because you might have helped
me escape?" suggested Daedalus.

Icarus stared hopelessly out of the high window. Doves circled the tower and he envied them their freedom. "If only we could fly," he sighed.

Daedalus looked up slowly from his book. "That's it," he murmured, then started sketching frantically.

Icarus recognized the glint in his father's eye. "What are you inventing now?" he asked.

"Wings!" came Daedalus' reply. "We're going to fly away from this island. But first we need lots of feathers..."

Over the months that followed, Daedalus and Icarus collected all the stray bird feathers they could lay their hands on. Each day, they used half their tiny bread ration to coax the birds onto the window ledge. Each night, they collected up the feathers and hid them under their mattresses. Gradually, the piles of feathers grew.

Daedalus was meticulous in his design.
Their lives depended on it. He stripped vines
from the tower walls and wove them into
frames for the wings, then he lined the frames
with his model-making wax. Carefully, he
pressed the feathers into the wax, arranging
them from smallest to largest and making
sure each feather overlapped the one beside it.

Strapping a pair to his back, Daedalus tried
a few wing beats. They lifted him into the
air, where he hovered triumphantly. Then he
strapped the other pair to his son.

"Are you sure they're strong enough?"
asked Icarus anxiously.

"So long as you don't fly too high or too
low," replied Daedalus. "Otherwise the
sun might melt the wax and the sea might
dampen the feathers."

Tentatively, Icarus clambered onto the
window ledge, took a deep breath and leaped.

He was gliding on the wind, more majestic
than any bird, leaving his prison behind him
and flying to freedom.

"Keep steady now," called Daedalus,
appearing beside his son. "I'll go in front, you
just follow me."

But Icarus was gaining in confidence. He
felt superhuman, invincible; he could fly like
the gods! Moving his outstretched arms, he
began to swoop and swerve. He dived down to
touch the waves, then soared up into the sky.

"Come back!" called Daedalus.

But Icarus was enjoying himself far too much to listen to his father. Looping the loop he flew on, soaring higher still.

Icarus didn't realize that the sun was melting the wax in his wings. He didn't notice his feathers floating off one by one. Daedalus shouted a warning and tried to reach his son, but by now he was just a speck in the sky. Then the speck started falling...

...and falling...

...until it disappeared

into the vast, blue sea.

Sir Gawain and the Green Knight

Centuries ago, King Arthur ruled from Camelot, helped by his noble knights. One New Year's Eve, a party was in full swing, when a giant man on horseback arrived at the castle. The knights stared, flabbergasted. Apart from his red, flashing eyes, the stranger was green... his skin, hair, beard and clothes. Even his horse was green. In one hand he carried a massive sword; the other held a holly bough.

"I'm here to find the bravest, most honest
knight," he roared. "Who will play my game?
Cut off my head now, and in a year and a day,
meet me in the Green Chapel that I may
return the blow."

There was a horrified
silence. Only Gawain, the
youngest knight, sprang
to his feet. "I accept your
challenge," he said.

With one thrust of his
sword, he beheaded
the Green Knight.

As the head rolled to the ground,
the Green Knight picked it up and put it
under his arm. Pale green lips repeated,
"Don't forget... the Green Chapel... in a year
and a day," and off the headless stranger rode.

Gawain kept his word, though he knew it
meant certain death.

He spent months searching the kingdom for the Green Chapel. Finally, starving and exhausted, he stumbled into a castle only three days before the time was up.

The castle belonged to Sir Bertilak and his lovely wife.

"The Green Chapel is very near," Bertilak said. "Stay until you fight the Green Knight. We'll make a bargain: every night, I'll give you a prize from my hunting, if you tell me what you've done while I've been out."

"Agreed!" laughed Gawain.

 On the first night, when Bertilak came home, Gawain confessed, "I kissed your wife once," and Bertilak gave him a deer.

"I kissed her twice," he said on the second night, and Bertilak gave him a boar.

"Three kisses today," he admitted on the third night, and Bertilak gave him a fox.

Gawain had told only half the truth. Bertilak's wife had given him a magic belt to keep him from harm. On New Year's Day, with the belt tied around his waist, and a quaking heart, he entered the Green Chapel.

"So! You have come!" cried the Green Knight, raising his sword as Gawain bared his neck, awaiting the fatal blow. The blade merely bruised his flesh.

The knight struck again. This time there

was a graze. The third time, the Green Knight cut into Gawain's neck but made only a small wound.

Then, as he flung down his sword...

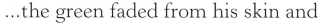

...the green faded from his skin and
hair, and Gawain saw that
in front of him stood
not the mysterious
Green Knight, but
Sir Bertilak.

"You've won my game
of honesty and bravery," Sir Bertilak smiled.
"You are a worthy knight."

"I wasn't honest," Gawain blurted out.
"And I'm a coward. I never told you that your
wife gave me a magic belt."

"You were brave enough. Return to King
Arthur's Court with your head held high."

"I'll wear the belt forever as a mark of
shame," swore Gawain, but King Arthur
admired his courage. From then on, all the
knights wore green belts to show their respect
for the youngest but bravest knight.

The Goose Girl

Princess Grace had promised to marry Prince Will. There was just one problem... they had never met. So today she was visiting him for the first time.

Before Grace left, her mother handed her a silver locket.

"It's magic," said the Queen. "It will protect you, so promise not to lose it."

"I promise," said Grace. She and her maid, Mona, climbed on their horses and set off.

It was a long, hard ride, and a blistering hot day. After a while, they came to a river.

"I'm thirsty," said Grace. "Please would you

pass my cup, Mona?"

"I didn't bother to pack it,"
snapped her maid. "I brought
mine, though." She filled her own
cup with water and gulped it down.

Grace lay on the hard ground and cupped
some water in her hands. As she did, her
locket chain came loose.

"Oh no!" cried Grace, as the locket
splashed into the water and was washed away.

"I'm going to tell your mother you lost the
locket," said Mona, laughing.

"Please don't," begged Grace. "I promised
her I'd take care of it."

"I'll keep quiet if you give me your clothes
and horse," said Mona. "And promise not to
tell a living thing we changed places."

Grace's horse, Falada, was not impressed.
And, since he could talk, he said so. "That's
horrible of you, Mona!"

But Grace had no choice. In silence, she exchanged her pretty gown for her maid's scruffy dress. Riding each other's horses, they continued their journey to Prince Will's palace.

When they arrived, Will ran up to Mona. "Welcome! You must be Princess Grace?"

"Yes," lied Mona. "This messy little thing is my maid. Give her a job that keeps her out of my way."

"She could help Conrad look after the geese," suggested Will's father, the King.

The very next morning,
Grace started her new job.
On the way to the meadow
where the geese were kept,
she saw Falada tied up to a tree.

"Poor Princess," he sighed.

Conrad was shocked. He'd never
heard a talking horse before. "Why
did he call you 'Princess'?" he asked.

But Grace couldn't say.

That night, Conrad told the King what
had happened. The King found Grace in the
kitchen. "Are you really a princess?" he asked.

"I promised not to tell a living thing," said
Grace, with a sigh.

The King thought. "Then tell this
cupboard," he suggested.

Grace climbed inside and recited the whole
sad story.

Outside, the King heard every word.

When Grace emerged, the King had her dressed in a gorgeous gown. Then he took her to the dining hall and sat her next to Will.

"Why is my maid sitting in my place?" barked Mona when she saw Grace.

"First, answer me this," replied the King. "What would you do with someone who was mean, rude and told lies?"

"Ha!" grinned Mona. "I'd stick them in a smelly barrel and roll them around the town."

"Good," said the King. "Then that's just what we'll do with you."

So mean Mona got what she deserved. Falada was freed. And Princess Grace married Prince Will, just as she had promised.

Snow White and the Seven Dwarfs

There was once a Queen who longed for a baby. One winter's day, she sat sewing by her window watching feathery snowflakes fall from the sky. Her needle slipped, three drops of blood fell on the snow and she dreamed of a daughter as white as the snow, with lips as red as blood, and hair as black as ebony.

Sadly, the Queen died just as her wish came true. Her baby, Snow White, was beautiful.

Soon after, the King re-married. His new Queen was dazzling but proud. Her fondest possession was a magic mirror, which she visited daily to ask:

"Mirror, mirror on the wall, who's the fairest of us all?"

"You," the mirror always replied, until one day it sang: "Lovely you are, it's true. But Snow White is lovelier than you."

"NOOOO!" screamed the Queen. "Then Snow White must die!" and she called for a huntsman. "Take the girl to the forest and kill her," she snarled.

The huntsman took Snow White deep into the forest, but he couldn't bear to hurt her. "Run!" he ordered, and Snow White fled.

Losing herself among the trees, she came to a strange little cottage, furnished with seven beds, seven chairs and a table laid with seven plates and seven cups.

The cottage belonged
to seven kind dwarfs,
who were shocked to hear
Snow White's story.

"Stay with us," they said.
"You'll be safe here."

The Queen, sure that Snow White was
dead, asked her mirror, "Who's fairest now?"

"Lovely you are, it's true. But Snow White
is lovelier than you," it answered.

"Never!" raged the Queen. She disguised
herself as an old woman and searched the
kingdom for Snow White, tracking her down
at last. She waited until the dwarfs had left for
work, before calling, "Pretty ribbons for sale!"

Snow White came running. "I'd like one,
to lace my dress," she said.

"Let me tie it for you," grinned the Queen,
pulling the ribbon tightly and squeezing all
the breath from Snow White's body.

When the dwarfs came home, they found Snow White lying on the ground. Horrified, they rushed to untie her.

Meanwhile, the Queen was back at her mirror. "Who's the fairest of us all?" she asked.

"Lovely you are, it's true. But Snow White is lovelier than you," came the reply.

Burning with anger, the Queen put on a new disguise and returned to the cottage. This time, she offered Snow White a comb, which she had secretly laced with poison.

As the comb touched Snow White's gleaming black hair, the poison entered her body and she collapsed.

The dwarfs discovered her slumped in a corner and feared the worst.

"Is she dead?" sobbed one.

"Not quite," said another, spotting the comb and whipping it out. Snow White was cured.

The Queen had raced home to her mirror. "Am I the fairest *now*?" she demanded.

Still the mirror replied, "Snow White is lovelier than you."

"She will not escape me!" vowed the Queen.

She took a red apple, halved it and dipped it in poison. Then she stuck it to half a green apple, disguised herself as a farmer's wife, and visited Snow White once more.

"Would you like to try a delicious apple?" she asked.

Snow White shook her head. "I can't."

"I promise it's harmless," said the Queen, taking a bite from the green half. "Eat," she urged.

Snow White sank her teeth into the red half

and fell lifelessly to the ground. This time,
even the dwarfs could not save her.

Weeping, they laid her
in a glass coffin, so
they could gaze at
her beauty forever.
There she might
have stayed but a
prince, riding by, fell in
love with her still, perfect face.

He lifted the coffin, and the piece of apple
fell from Snow White's mouth. She coughed
and began to breathe, opening her eyes to see
her handsome rescuer.

The Queen, furious beyond measure to hear
Snow White had come back to life, exploded in
a fit of jealousy. Blissfully unaware
of this, Snow White married
her prince and lived happily –
and safely – ever after.

The Milkmaid

It was early in the morning when Daisy set off for the market, carrying two pails of milk on a yoke across her shoulders. She was on her way to sell it, and as she walked along, she began to daydream.

"When I sell this milk, I'll get some money," she thought, "and with that money, I'll buy a nice plump hen. My hen will lay some eggs... lots and lots of eggs!"

"I can sell the eggs to the parson's wife. Then I'll have more money... lots and lots and lots of it!

I'll buy more hens and sell more eggs and soon I'll be rich. I'll be able to buy myself a beautiful new dress, and a new coat, and maybe a pair of shoes. Lots of shoes! Pink ones and blue ones and green ones...

I'll have so many lovely things that there won't be room for them in Tumbledown Cottage, so I'll have to move to a big, fancy house. And I'll have servants to take care of me: a butler, a maid, a cook, and someone to take care of the hens, of course...

I'll look so beautiful in my new clothes, that soon enough a prince will fall head over heels in love with me..."

"He'll be the perfect prince – good, clever, handsome, kind and incredibly rich.

Of course, we'll get married. I'll be a princess! We'll have lots of dances at our wedding. He'll be a wonderful dancer. He'll twirl and whirl me around – like this..."

Daisy whirled and twirled in the market place. As she did, the yoke slipped and the milk poured out onto the street.

"My milk!" Daisy cried, looking down at her empty buckets.

"Cheer up!" said a passing farmer. "There's no point crying over spilt milk."

The Gingerbread Man

Once upon a time, a little old woman and a little old man lived in a little old cottage in a faraway land.

One day, the little old woman decided to make a man out of gingerbread. She mixed and she stirred and she made some dough. She kneaded and stretched it and cut out a shape. Then she put on two raisins for eyes, a raisin mouth and three raisin buttons, and popped him in the oven to bake.

After a while, there was a tap at the oven door. "Let me out! Let me out!"

The little old woman opened the oven door in

surprise, and out jumped the gingerbread man. He ran across the floor and straight out through the open door.

"Come back!" cried the little old woman and the little old man. "We want to eat you."

But the gingerbread man ran on down the garden path, crying, "Run! Run! As fast as you can. You can't catch me, I'm the gingerbread man!"

The gingerbread man ran on, past a horse and a cow in a meadow.

"Come here!" neighed the horse. "We want to eat you."

But the gingerbread man ran on down the road singing, "I've run away from a little old woman and a little old man and I can run away from you too, yes I can!"

Run! Run! As fast as you can.

You can't catch me, I'm the gingerbread man!

The gingerbread man ran past a farmer in his field.

"Come here!" cried the farmer. "I want to eat you."

But the gingerbread man ran on down the road singing, "I've run away from a horse and a cow, a little old woman and a little old man and I can run away from you too, yes I can!"

Run! Run! As fast as you can.

You can't catch me, I'm the gingerbread man!

Next, the gingerbread man ran past a school full of children.

"Stop, stop! Come here!" they called. "We want to eat you."

But the gingerbread man ran on down the

road singing, "I've run away from a farmer, a horse and a cow, a little old woman and a little old man and I can run away from you too, yes I can!"

Run! Run! As fast as you can.

You can't catch me, I'm the gingerbread man!

Then the gingerbread man came to a river. He couldn't go back or he'd be caught. He couldn't go forward or he'd get wet and melt.

"I can help," said a fox, seeing his panic and creeping towards him. "Climb on my back and I'll carry you across the river."

"Thank you!" said the gingerbread man, and he jumped onto the fox's tail.

The fox began swimming across the river. "Oh dear," he said. "My tail is dragging in the water. Better climb on my back."

The gingerbread man climbed up the fox's back.

"Oh dear," said the fox again. "Now my back is getting wet. Why not climb onto my head?"

The gingerbread man gingerly climbed onto the fox's head.

The fox tossed his head. The gingerbread man flew into the air... and SNAP! The gingerbread man was a quarter gone. SNAP! went the fox again, and the gingerbread man was half gone. SNAP! went the fox and the gingerbread man was three quarters gone.

SNAP! SNAP! CRUNCH! went the fox and that was the end of the gingerbread man.

How Bear Lost His Tail

Back in the old days, Bear had the most magnificent, long, bushy tail. He loved his tail, and so did all the other animals... except Fox. Now, Fox had a long, bushy tail of his own. He didn't like the way Bear showed off and got all the attention, so he decided to play a trick on him.

One winter's day, he stole a few fish that a fisherman had caught and carried them to an ice hole in the lake. When Bear smelled them, he lumbered over.

"What delicious fish," he said to Fox.

"I can show you how to catch them if you like," replied crafty Fox.

Bear nodded hungrily.

"Of course, only animals with wonderful tails like ours can catch fish in this way," Fox went on. "You just sit on the ice with your back to the hole and dangle your wonderfully long tail into the water. When a fish nibbles at your fur, simply whip your tail out of the water."

"But how will I know when that is?" asked Bear. "I might not feel it."

"I'll hide close by," Fox promised, "and shout 'Now!' when the time is right."

The hungry bear sat down eagerly and dipped his tail into the chilly water.

"It may take some time," warned Fox.

"Keep very still, and don't pull your tail out until I say so."

With that, sly Fox sneaked off and hid. He spied on Bear for a while, to make sure he was doing as he was told. Then he trotted home to his warm lair, leaving Bear alone on the ice.

Bear waited and waited.

Day became night.

The night grew colder.

It began to snow.

Tired and hungry, Bear slumped down on the ice and fell asleep.

The following morning, Fox woke up and thought of Bear. "I wonder if he's still there..."

Fox trotted back to the hole in the ice but all he could see was a little white hill with two ears sticking out. He crept closer... and heard Bear snoring under a mound of snow.

Rascally Fox giggled in amusement, then crept even closer and yelled at the top of his voice, "NOW!"

Poor Bear woke in a fluster and yanked at his tail. SNAP! He turned to see the tasty fish he had caught, but saw instead his magnificent tail trapped in the ice. The hole had frozen over in the night and his tail had completely broken off. "I'm so sorry," Fox cried, quickly scampering away. "I had no idea something like that would happen."

Bear glowered after Fox. "I'll get you for this!" he roared.

And that is why, to this day, bears have short stubby tails... and no love of foxes.

The Tin Soldier

"Happy birthday, Ben," said his dad, handing him a brightly covered box.

Ben excitedly unwrapped his present. "Tin soldiers?" he shouted. "Just what I wanted. Thanks Dad!"

 His dad noticed that one of the soldiers only had one leg. Ben didn't care.

He spent all day marching his new toys around his room. But when bedtime came, he couldn't see the one-legged soldier anywhere.

"Never mind," said Dad. "You can look for him tomorrow."

While Ben was asleep, something magical happened. All his toys sprang to life, and

ran around his bedroom
playing games.

The lost soldier had fallen
behind some building blocks.
Peeking out, he saw a beautiful
ballerina dancing on one leg.

"She'd be the perfect wife
for me," he thought. He smiled
at the paper doll. She smiled back.

"Keep your eyes to yourself, soldier!"
snapped the jealous jack-in-the-box.

The next morning, Ben found the soldier
and put him on the window sill.

"Now's my chance," thought the wicked
jack-in-the-box. He took a deep breath and
blew the tin soldier through the open window.

The soldier fell onto the street below. At
that moment, two boys rushed up.

"Hey, a soldier!" shouted one.

"Let's make him a sailor," laughed the other.

They folded a boat out of newspaper, put the soldier inside and sent the boat sailing along the gutter.

"Ha, ha!" laughed one boy. "Watch him go!"

Seconds later, the boat fell down a drain hole and landed, *plop*, in a dark, smelly sewer.

"Whew, what a stink," thought the soldier, as the boat drifted through the dirty water. Just then, he saw a sinister figure scuttling in the shadows up ahead and a fat, dirty rat jumped out at him.

"Pay me a penny to pass!" it demanded.

"Sorry, no money," said the soldier, as he sailed by. "Oh dear," he thought, and gave a sad sigh. "I wonder if I'll ever see the pretty ballerina doll again?"

Before long, he spotted daylight. The boat
whooshed out of the sewer and splash-landed
in a swirling river below.

The soldier only just had time to catch
his breath, before he realized
his little boat was sinking.

But even worse was
to come...

A huge fish
swam along and
gobbled him up,
chomp, in one bite.

"I'll be stuck inside
this fish forever," sniffed
the soldier. But his luck was about
to change, for a while at least.

That afternoon, a fisherman caught the
fish. "What a beauty!" he thought, and took it
to the market to sell.

Then, who should buy the fish but Ben's

dad? He carried the fish home, unwrapped it and out fell the tin soldier. He rushed into Ben's room. "Look who's back!"

Ben was delighted.

The ballerina was overjoyed to see the tin soldier again too, but the jack-in-the-box was furious. That night, he waited until the soldier was standing by the fireplace, and blew him into the flames.

The ballerina couldn't bear to be parted from her brave soldier, so she fluttered into the fire to be by his side.

The next morning, Ben saw that both toys were missing. What's more, in the ashes of the fire he found a shiny silver sequin and a tiny tin heart.

He never discovered how they came to be there. But he kept them safely together forever.

The Fisherman and the Genie

Once, a young fisherman lived by a river. Each day, he strung his nets across the rushing water, and each evening, he came home with a basketful of plump, silvery fish.

But, on this particular day, he wasn't having much luck. "Where are all the fish?" he sighed, poking at a net full of muddy stones.

Something glinted in the mud. "A fish!" he thought hopefully. But it wasn't. It was an old blue bottle, tightly sealed. "I wonder what's inside?" He shook it, but he couldn't hear anything. So he yanked out the stopper – *pop!* – and looked down the neck of the bottle.

Still nothing.

He was about to throw it away when smoke began pouring out, billowing and blowing into strange shapes... two eyes... a mouth...

"A genie!" gasped the fisherman, backing away in terror.

"Yes," boomed the genie. "And I've been trapped in that bottle for centuries. Now I'm longing for something to eat! Mmm, you look tasty." His powerful hand reached out.

"Wait..." cried the fisherman, thinking fast. "Did you just come out of that bottle?"

"Yes," snapped the genie.

"I don't believe it," said the fisherman. "How on earth did you fit?"

"I can do *anything*," said the genie. "Look, I'll show you – and *then* I'll eat you up."

He whooshed back into the bottle...
...and the fisherman jammed in the stopper.
   "And there you'll stay," he told the bottle
sternly, "until you learn not to eat people!"

The Baobab Tree

So long ago that no one can remember when, the gods made the world. First, they made the land and sea, then mountains and plains. One day, they made a tree that could talk and named it the Baobab tree.

Alone in the dry soil, the Baobab tree was far from happy. "It's too hot," it complained. "I'm thirsty," it moaned.

The gods ignored the Baobab tree and grew a forest of tall palms.

"It's not fair," grumbled the Baobab tree. "Why am I so short? Why can't I be taller?"

The gods continued to ignore the discontented Baobab and created trees with beautiful, bright flowers.

"Why can't
I have pretty
flowers," whined
the Baobab tree.

By now, the gods
were losing patience.

"Just be quiet, will you?" they urged
the Baobab tree. "Can't you see we have
work to do?"

This time, they were growing trees
with delicious, juicy fruits.

"Hey, why do *they* get fancy fruits?"
called out the Baobab tree. "I want some too."

"That's enough!" shouted the gods.

"All you do is complain. Can't
you be quiet for even one
moment?"

"But it's simply not
fair," huffed the Baobab
tree, scowling.

"That does it," said the chief god. He conferred with the others, then turned on the Baobab tree. "If you can't stop talking," he announced, "we'll have to make you."

"No! Wait!" cried the Baobab tree, but it was powerless against the gods.

They wrenched it from the soil, flipped it upside down, and planted its head and branches deep under the earth. Only its trunk and roots were visible above ground, and its voice was heard no more.

That is how the Baobab tree still looks today... and now you know why.

The Tortoise and the Eagle

"I wish I could fly," said the little tortoise, to nobody in particular. She was gazing up at the birds, soaring through the sky above her. "If only I could be so fast, so graceful and so free."

As she said these words, an eagle landed on the ground beside her.

"You want to fly?" he asked.

"More than anything!" she replied.

"But you don't have feathers or wings," said the eagle. "You're made for the Earth."

"I'm sure I could fly, if I just had the chance," the tortoise insisted.

"If I teach you to fly," the eagle began, "what will you give me in return?"

"You can have everything I own!" offered the tortoise, who kept many treasures in her shell.

"Well, if you're sure," the eagle said.

"Of course I am!" said the tortoise. "What are we waiting for?"

So the eagle picked up the little tortoise in his big black claws, flapped his wings, and took off.

The Earth disappeared beneath the tortoise, and the wind rushed past her ears. Suddenly, they were flying high above the fields.

"Are you ready to fly?" asked the eagle.

"Yes! Yes I am!"

At that, the eagle let her go, and the tortoise dropped through the air like a stone.

"I wish I'd stayed on land," she wailed as she plummeted. "I wasn't made to fly!"

She landed on a patch of springy moss with a bump. Lying there, dazed, bruised and shaken, she saw the eagle circling overhead.

"I'll stick to what I can do from now on," she decided.

The Peach Boy

Many years ago, a poor, elderly couple lived in Japan. One day, the old woman was down at the river, washing her husband's socks, when she saw a giant peach drifting by. Delighted, she yanked it out with a bamboo cane and rolled it home to eat.

When they cut the peach in half, the couple gasped in shock – for out hopped a little boy.

"Let's call him Momotaro," said the old man. "Little Peachling."

They loved him like a son and he grew up to be the strongest, bravest young man in the village, but Momotaro found life too quiet. He yearned for adventure.

"I shall sail across the sea to the Island of Monsters," he decided.

"I wish you wouldn't go," said his mother, but Momotaro had made up his mind. With a sigh, the old woman packed some of her home-made millet dumplings in his leather pouch. "To eat on the journey," she said.

Momotaro waved his parents goodbye and set off. He hadn't been walking long, when a dog came sniffing up.

"What's that I can smell in your pouch?" the dog barked, drooling.

"Tasty dumplings," Momotaro replied, "to eat on my way to the Island of Monsters."

"If you give me one, I'll come with you," said the dog.

Feeling in need of company, Momotaro took out a millet dumpling and tossed it to him.

A while later, a curious monkey swung down from the treetops.

"What's that I can smell in your pouch?"
he asked, licking his lips.

Momotaro told him about the millet
dumplings and the monkey offered to join
them in exchange for one. Once more,
Momotaro agreed.

Soon after, a pheasant swooped down
from the sky. He wanted a dumpling too. So
Momotaro fed him one of the treats, and
together the four continued on their way to
the coast.

Momotaro found a little wooden boat,
and they rowed across the choppy waters
to the forbidding Island
of Monsters.

In the middle of the island
stood a vast fortress with
mighty wooden doors.
Momotaro heaved them
open and strode inside.

From out of the shadows scuttled the monsters' hideous goblin servants. They reached out to grab Momotaro, but he fought them back with his sword.

The four friends charged into the next chamber. This was the throne room of the monsters. The animals gasped at the sight of Akandoji, the terrible king of the monsters, who leaped up and stood towering over them.

"Who dares to enter my domain?" roared Akandoji.

"I do," declared Momotaro bravely. "And I'm not scared of you."

Snarling and growling, the giant monster lashed out with his hefty sword. But Momotaro was too quick for him, blocking every blow the creature made.

Meanwhile, the dog, the monkey and the pheasant nipped and pecked at the Monster King from all angles.

Eventually, the breathless beast lay exhausted at Momotaro's feet.

"Leave me in peace!" he begged. "Take my jewels if you must. Just go!"

Momotaro grabbed a sackful of precious stones and gold from an enormous treasure chest and ran from the fortress.

The four adventurers returned to the village as heroes, and the elderly couple were never poor again, thanks to the brave, adventurous Peach Boy.

The Billy Goats Gruff

The three Billy Goats Gruff were hungry. They wanted to reach the lush mountain grass on the other side of the river.

Unfortunately, first they had to cross a bridge, and under this bridge there lived a great, ugly troll. He had eyes as wide as saucers, a nose as long as a poker and a huge appetite for juicy billy goats.

WARNING: GOATS BEWARE!

"Me first," said the youngest, smallest billy goat when they reached the bridge.

Trip trap trip trap went his hooves on the wooden slats. Then a booming voice made the whole bridge shudder.

"Who's that trip-trapping over my bridge?"

"It's only me, the smallest Billy Goat Gruff, crossing over to reach the lush grass."

"Oh no you're not," roared the voice. "I'm coming to gobble you up." And the ghastly troll heaved himself up onto the bridge.

"No! No! Don't eat me," begged the little billy goat. "My brother's coming next. Why don't you wait for him? He's much bigger and juicier than me."

The troll reluctantly agreed and slunk back under the bridge, leaving the little billy goat to gambol towards the tasty grass beyond.

Moments later, the second, larger billy goat came *trip trap trip trap* across the wooden slats.

"Who's that trip-trapping over my bridge?" boomed the fearsome troll.

"It's only me, the middle-sized Billy Goat Gruff, crossing over to reach the lush grass."

"Oh no you're not," roared the troll, heaving himself back onto the bridge. "I'm going to gobble you up."

"No! No! Don't eat me," cried the second billy goat. "My big brother's coming next and he's even bigger and juicier than  me. You should definitely wait for him."

The troll agreed, even more reluctantly, and slunk back under the bridge, leaving the second billy goat to trot over to the tasty grass.

Not long after, the third, even larger billy goat came *TRIP TRAP TRIP TRAP* across the wooden slats.

"Who's that trip-trapping over my bridge?" boomed the troll with glee.

"It's me, the biggest Billy Goat Gruff."

"Then I'm coming to gobble you up," roared the troll, clambering onto the bridge.

"Oh no you're not," replied the third billy goat, lowering his horns and charging at the troll. With a toss of his head, he flung the ugly troll into the rushing water below. As the troll floated away down the river, the largest Billy Goat Gruff of all stomped off to join his brothers in the lush, mountain grass.

The Three Wishes

An old farmer lived with his wife in a small farmhouse. One day, he was in his wheat field, swinging his scythe, when he heard a faint cry. Looking closer, he saw a fairy, trembling between the stalks of wheat.

"Please help!" cried her small voice. "My wings are trapped and I can't fly."

"Of course," replied the farmer, gently pulling the stalks apart.

The fairy flew free and hovered before him. "Thank you," she said. "In return, I shall grant you three wishes."

Then, with a twirl, she disappeared.

The farmer rushed home, his mind racing with all the things he could wish for.

"You won't believe it!" he called out to his wife. "I rescued a fairy and now we have three wishes!"

"Well I never," declared the farmer's wife. He was home early and she hadn't yet had time to prepare their evening meal. "I wish I had a sausage," she murmured.

In an instant, a large sausage appeared on the table.

"A sausage?" cried the farmer. "What a ridiculous thing to wish for! I wish that sausage was on the end of your nose."

And, in an instant, it was.

"Agghhh!" shrieked his wife, shaking her head and running around in circles. "Get this thing off me!" she yelled.

The farmer grabbed the sausage and tugged with all his might. He pulled so hard that his wife's head nearly came off, but the sausage wouldn't move.

By now, the farmer's wife was in tears and the farmer was feeling very foolish.

"What are we going to do?" she sobbed.

The farmer looked at her, with her ludicrous sausage nose, and suddenly grinned. "We still have one more wish," he said. "I wish that sausage was off your nose."

In an instant, it was.

His wife jumped for joy and the farmer hugged her with relief.

"We've run out of wishes," she pointed out.

"I know," he replied, "but at least we have a sausage for supper!"

Tom Thumb

Once, there was a farmer's wife who
longed for a son. "Even if he is no bigger
than my thumb," she sighed.

A kind fairy must have heard her, for that
night a beautiful flower sprang up below her
window – and when its petals opened, she
found a tiny boy curled up inside.

"Let's call him Tom," she whispered to
her husband. She was delighted with her son,
although his size did get him into trouble.

One day, Tom was
picking berries when a bird
flew up. A moment later,
he and his berry were high
in the sky. "Let go!" he yelled.

Startled, the bird did so. Tom tumbled
down – *splash* – into a river. A huge fish
opened its mouth, and everything went dark.

That afternoon, a cook cut open the fish in
the palace kitchen and out popped Tom. She
was so surprised, she carried him to the King.

"Whatever were you doing in my dinner?"
he exclaimed.

So Tom explained: "...and the fish was
caught by a fisherman, and here I am!"

"What a story!" said the King. "You should
be made a knight." And he gave Tom a needle
for a sword, and a tame mouse to ride.

Tom was riding around the throne room,
when a maid screamed. "Aargh, a rat!"

Tom wasn't afraid. "*Charge!*" He galloped over, brandishing his needle, and the rat fled.

The King laughed. "Such bravery deserves a reward," he told Tom, opening a chest full of treasure. "Take what you can carry."

Tom stared open-mouthed at the heaps of heavy gold and jewels. Then he spotted a little silver penny. "I'd like that," he said. "Thank you, your Majesty! Now I must go. My mother will be worried."

It was almost midnight by the time Tom rode up to the familiar farmhouse.

"Tom!" cried his parents, relieved to see him again. "Where have you been?"

"On an adventure," replied Tom. "I met the King and made my fortune." He showed them the penny. "But ah, it's good to be home!"

The Magic Gifts

There was once a rich merchant who had three sons – Sang, Kang and Chung.

Just before he died, the old man made his sons promise to share his fortune equally.

But when the fateful day came, Sang and Kang went back on their promise. They sold everything their father owned, including his house, and divided the money between them.

"You can have this tiny bag of coins, little brother," Sang told Chung.

"And think yourself lucky," added Kang.

Sang and Kang bought themselves a big, fancy house and filled it with expensive furniture.

Poor Chung could only afford a hut in the nearby village.

One day, he was in the forest, looking for something to eat, when he met a wizened old monk carrying a huge bundle of bamboo.

"Please could you help me over the stream?" the monk croaked. "The bridge has broken and I can't get home."

"I'll take you across," said Chung. Puffing and panting, he carried the monk and his load across the stream.

When they reached the monk's lonely mountain home, Chung felt sorry for the old man, so he offered to stay and take care of him.

The monk was delighted. But, after a few weeks, it was clear to him that Chung was missing his family and friends.

"I'm grateful for all your help," said the monk, "but it's time you went home. I have a little something to thank you for being so kind." He reached into his robe and handed Chung a straw mat. Wrapped inside was a wooden spoon and a pair of chopsticks.

Chung headed off, but night soon came on and he lost his way in the dark.

"I'll have to spend the night here," he thought, spreading the mat on the hard ground. "I just wish I was more comfortable," he sighed, as he tried to get to sleep.

When he woke, he found he was inside a luxurious castle, lying on the biggest, softest

bed he had ever slept on. Under the mattress was his straw mat.

"This mat must be magic!" he thought.

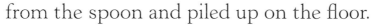

He picked up the
spoon. "I wish I had
some food to eat
with this."

At that moment,
masses of fruit cascaded
from the spoon and piled up on the floor.

Chung took the chopsticks and gave them
a tap. Four lovely dancing girls magically
appeared, singing sweet songs as he ate.

Not long after, Chung's brothers were
passing the castle. They had never noticed it
before. Curious, they went inside.

"Chung!" they cried in amazement when
they saw their brother and his new riches.

Chung told them all about the old monk.

"Perhaps if we were poor, the monk would
give us magic gifts," whispered Sang to Kang.

So the two brothers gave away all their
possessions, including their fancy house.

With nothing but the clothes on their backs, they marched to the monk's home. The old man was nowhere to be seen.

"Let's wait for him," suggested Sang.

So they waited... and waited... and waited...

A year went by and the brothers were still waiting. Fed up and bedraggled, they trudged back to Chung's castle.

"We're sorry we were so mean to you," sniffed Sang. "It's no fun being poor."

"Please forgive us," begged Kang.

"Of course I will," said Chung. "A happy family is the best gift of all."

The Sun and the Wind

High up in the sky, the Wind and the Sun were arguing. They had known each other for many years, and they never agreed about anything.

"I am more powerful than you," the Wind puffed.

"I disagree," said the Sun, smiling gently.

"Of course I am," the Wind roared. "When I blow, I create storms! I can make hurricanes and tornadoes! I can destroy a city in a few moments, if I choose."

The Sun shrugged.

"If you don't believe me," the Wind went on, "then watch this!"

He took a deep breath, flew down towards the ocean, and blew out an enormous gust of air. Soon waves as tall as towers were racing towards the beach nearby.

As the waves rolled towards the shore, all the boats at sea were thrown into the air as if they were tiny toys. The waves smashed onto the beach, scattering people in all directions. Dogs barked, roofs rattled and doors slammed. The Wind kept blowing, and soon all the trees were stripped of their leaves. Finally, the Wind stopped.

"You see?" he said proudly, only slightly out of breath. "I am more powerful than you."

"You have the power to destroy," said the Sun. "But that's not the only kind of power."

The Sun shone brightly and soon people on the Earth below were walking through the streets, enjoying the warmth on their faces.

"People love me," said the Sun. "They only fear you."

"I am still more powerful than you," huffed the Wind, "and I'm going to prove it. Let's settle this once and for all."

The Wind looked down to the Earth, and spotted a man walking briskly along a country lane. "Whoever makes him take his coat off is the most powerful," said the Wind.

He took a deep breath, blew with all his strength, and sent huge gusts whipping along the road. The man pulled his coat around him, and walked on.

So the Wind blew again, and this time, the trees creaked as they bent over. The Wind was howling, and the man's coat flew open but it stayed on. The incensed Wind blew once more.

This time he sent a blast so strong that branches snapped off the trees, and gusts roared down the road. The man rushed into a hut to take shelter.

The Wind looked down, furious and out of breath. "Your turn," he huffed to the Sun.

So the Sun began to shine. Moments later, the man poked his head out of the shelter. Soon, he was walking along the road and onto the beach. As the Sun shone down, the man took off his coat and his shoes and socks too.

The Wind was speechless with anger.

"Gentleness can be more powerful than force," said the Sun, but the Wind wasn't listening. He had whirled off into a rage, and was brewing up a hurricane.

Puss in Boots

O nce, a miller had three sons. The two eldest were selfish and greedy, but the youngest, Gabriel, was honest and kind.

When their father died, the eldest son inherited his mill and the middle son got his donkey. Gabriel was left with the cat.

"What shall I do?" he worried, stroking the cat and scratching its ears. "I have no money and no way of earning any..."

"Troubles can be a blessing in disguise," said the cat. "Buy me a stout pair of boots and a strong leather bag, and stop worrying."

"C-c-certainly," replied Gabriel, astounded that the cat could talk.

The next day Puss, wearing his shiny new boots, filled the leather bag with parsley and hid by a rabbit hole. Soon a fat rabbit crept inside. Quickly, Puss pounced, and carried it straight to the palace.

"A gift, Your Majesty," he declared, bowing low before the King, "from my noble master, the Marquis of Carabas."

"Please thank your master," said the astonished King.

The day after that, Puss caught two partridges and presented them to the King,

 who was thrilled by this generous Marquis and his gifts, and enormously impressed by his talking cat.

"I'm taking my daughter to drive along the river this afternoon," the King told Puss, who raced to find Gabriel.

"Hurry! We must go to the river at once!" Puss ordered.

Gabriel was baffled but followed his cat.

"Now," said Puss, as soon as they reached the riverbank, "undress, jump in the river and your fortune is made."

Gabriel was even more puzzled, and the water looked freezing, but Puss was so insistent that he did as he was told.

As Gabriel swam, and the King's carriage passed by, Puss bundled up Gabriel's clothes and hid them under a rock.

"Help!" he squealed. "My master was attacked by robbers. They threw him in the river and now he's drowning."

The King's servants rushed to help Gabriel from the water, while Puss explained to the King that the robbers had even stolen the Marquis' clothes.

"Luckily, I have a spare evening suit in my carriage," said the King, and Gabriel put it on. He looked wonderful in the King's finery and both the King and the princess admired the handsome, charming young man.

"Please, join us on our ride," said the King.

Meanwhile, Puss ran ahead to some fields, where men were reaping corn.

Showing his claws and baring his teeth, Puss snarled, "When the King passes, 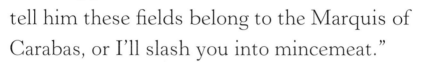 tell him these fields belong to the Marquis of Carabas, or I'll slash you into mincemeat."

Terrified, and believing that a talking cat could probably do anything, the men agreed.

Puss ran on, to where a group of shepherds were tending sheep, and hissed, "Say these pastures belong to the Marquis of Carabas or you're mincemeat."

He made woodsmen in the forest repeat the same words too.

When the King passed by in his carriage, he smiled broadly and murmured to Gabriel, "What a lot you own, Marquis."

By this time, Puss had reached a
magnificent castle where a fierce ogre lived.

"I hear," Puss began, "that you can turn
yourself into any number of beasts. Is that
really true?"

"YES!" roared the ogre, transforming
himself into a mighty lion. He shook his
golden mane and swiped at Puss
with a vicious paw.

"Wonderful!" said Puss,
skipping out of the way. "Truly
incredible. But I don't
suppose you could
become a *small*
animal... a
mouse, for
instance?"

"Watch me!" growled the ogre. Puss killed
the mouse with one blow just as the King's
carriage arrived at the gates.

"Welcome to the Marquis' castle," purred Puss, ushering the King, the princess and Gabriel through to the banqueting hall, where a grand feast had been laid out for the ogre.

"Will you marry my daughter, Marquis?" asked the King, enchanted by all this wealth.

"I'd be delighted to, if she'll have me," Gabriel replied, "but I should tell you that I'm only a miller's son, not a Marquis... I owe all of this to my cat."

"You are an honest man," said the King, "and as such, deserving of my daughter."

So the couple married and lived happily ever after, while the King, still in awe of Puss' cleverness, made him his Prime Minister.

Why the Sea is Salty

Long ago, the sea wasn't salty like it is today. Instead, it tasted fresh and sweet. So where did the salt come from? Well, it all began with a magic millstone...

This millstone belonged to a wealthy King. Whatever the King wanted – glittering gold coins, precious gems, or rare, exotic spices – he simply had to ask the millstone, and it would grind them out... until one night, a thief tiptoed into the palace and carried the millstone off.

The thief knew he would have to travel for miles to escape the King's anger, so he had left a boat stocked with food ready for his getaway. He raced to the shore, jumped in and set sail. Then, feeling hungry, he took out a dumpling.

"Pah, this needs salt," he spat, after one mouthful. "Hey, millstone – make some salt!"

At once, the millstone began to grind out sparkling white salt. The thief sprinkled a little on his dumpling, gobbled it up and fell asleep – without telling the stone to stop.

All night, the millstone kept grinding. By dawn, there was so much salt, the boat was sinking under the weight of it. A wave sloshed over the side, waking the thief.

"Uh-oh," he gasped.
"Where's that stone? I
have to stop it!"
Frantically, he
burrowed through
the salt – but the
millstone was buried
too deep.

The salt kept coming,
and the boat kept sinking, until it sank to the
bottom of the ocean. And there the millstone
has stayed, grinding out salt to this very day.

As for the thief, he had a long swim home –
and an angry King waiting to meet him.

The Fox and the Crow

Deep in the forest there lived a fox who was always hungry. One evening, he was trotting along, when he sniffed the air and caught the scent of something delicious. He pricked up his ears, heard a rustling coming from the tree above him and looked up, to see a little crow hopping along a branch. In the crow's beak was an enormous lump of cheese.

"Cheese?" thought the fox. "Delectable cheese! That's far too tasty to waste on a crow."

The fox cleared his throat "Hello, Miss Crow," he called, and the crow looked down.

"I hope you don't
mind me interrupting
you," the fox went on,
"but I couldn't help
noticing what a very
pretty bird you are."

He flashed her his most charming smile.

"How kind!" thought the crow, in surprise.
She wasn't used to animals talking to her,
especially foxes.

"You have such wonderfully glossy
feathers," said the fox.

"Glossy?" she thought. "My feathers?"

"They really are," said the fox. "And that
beautiful, long tail…"

"Is it?" thought the crow. She turned
around to look at her tail and nearly fell off
the branch in the process.

"You are simply the prettiest bird that I
have ever set eyes on," declared the fox.

The crow blushed.

"It's such a shame you can't sing," the fox went on. "If only you had a beautiful voice too... Well, that would be perfect."

"But I can sing!" the crow thought, hopping up and down on the branch. "I love singing!"

"Yes, if only you could sing," repeated the fox, with a sigh.

"I shall sing him a song right now!" thought the crow.

She ruffled her feathers, cleared her throat, shut her eyes and opened her beak as wide as she could.

The cheese went tumbling out of it, and the fox snapped up the cheese in his jaws.

"Caaawwwww..." went the crow.

"Delicious," murmured the fox.

"Caawww- hey! Wait! Where's my cheese?"

"Finders keepers," said the fox.

"But that was MY cheese," shouted the crow. "And what about my song? Did you like it?"

"Sorry, Crow," said the fox. "But you shouldn't always believe the nice things that people say to you. Sometimes they just want something from you."

The crow jumped up and down on her branch in fury. She vowed never to talk to another fox again. As for the fox, he sauntered off into the forest, licking his lips and smiling to himself.

The Frog Prince

The King's youngest, most beautiful daughter loved to play in the palace garden, throwing and catching her golden ball. One day, she dropped it. It rolled down the hill and sank into the depths of a pond.

"My golden ball," she wept, "lost forever!"

"I'll find it," croaked a frog.

The princess shuddered. She hated frogs. She didn't like their green, slimy skin. Or their bulging eyes. Or their wide mouths with such thin lips.

She could hardly bear to look at him, but she said, grimacing, "I'll give you pearls and diamonds if you do."

The frog shook his ugly head.

"I want to sit at your table, eat from your plate, drink from your cup and sleep in your bed. Will you promise me that?"

"I promise," she smiled, not meaning it. "I won't let him near me," she thought. "Ugh!" With a swirl of bubbles, the frog dived into the pond and returned, holding up the ball in triumph.

The princess snatched it from him and danced away. "Your promise..." he called, but she laughed. "You're dreaming, frog. Never, never, NEVER!"

Determinedly, he hopped after her. That evening, everyone at dinner heard a wet *splat-splat* on the stairs and a tap at the door.

In the silence that followed, a croaky
voice proclaimed, "Remember your promise,
youngest princess."

"Who's that?" asked the King.

"No one really," said the princess. "Only a
horrible frog who found my ball."

"What did you promise?"

"To share my plate," she muttered.

"A princess keeps her word," thundered
the King. "Do it NOW."

Reluctantly, the princess picked
up the frog and dumped him on
the table. She watched his wide-
stretched mouth murmur,
"Push your plate near,
so we may eat together.
And pass your cup."
She felt sick.
"I'm tired," the frog said
at last. "Take me up to bed."

The princess shut him in a drawer while she got ready for bed, ignoring his grumbling croaks. When she took him out again, she pictured him hopping all over her lovely clean sheets. It made her so angry that she opened her window and hurled him out onto the palace lawn.

"Now you'll be quiet, you horrible frog."

There was a thud... then silence.

The princess felt dreadful. "I've killed him," she wailed, racing outside. The frog lay face down, completely still.

Tears fell from her eyes. "I didn't really want you to die," she whispered, crouching down to give him a kiss.

The night shook with a roll of thunder like a thousand guns firing, and hundreds of stars lit up the sky. The frog vanished. In his place, a dazed prince wobbled before her.

"You've saved me!" he said, to the startled princess. "I was under a spell, cast by a wicked witch. It could only be broken with a kiss. Princess, in return for your kindness in kissing a frog, will you marry me?"

"I will when I grow up," she said. And this promise, unlike her last, she was more than happy to keep.

How Zebras Got Their Stripes

Long ago, when this story begins, the world had just one zebra. And he wasn't black-and-white striped, like zebras today. Apart from his jet black mane, this zebra was creamy white all over.

He lived with a giraffe, an elephant and a greedy baboon, beside a deep pond.

They should have been perfectly happy but the baboon was a selfish creature, who flatly refused to share the pond with any of them.

"This is my pond!" he declared. "You can all keep away." And he would dance a splashy dance and guzzle the delicious water.

The others grew angry.

"But we're thirsty," they said, "and there's plenty of water."

"Don't care," said Baboon rudely. "You're not getting any."

That afternoon, Giraffe crept to the pond.

Baboon roared at him. "GO AWAY!" he yelled, jumping up and down and waving his arms in the air.

Giraffe fled.

Next, Elephant lumbered over to the pond.

Before the tip of his trunk could touch the water, Baboon leaped out from behind a tree.

"GO AWAY!" he hollered, jumping up and down and beating his fists on his chest.

At last, Zebra walked up.

"GO AWAY!" Baboon yelled.

Zebra ignored him and stamped a hoof. "It's NOT your pond," he said. "It belongs to all of us and you must share it."

"No!" said Baboon. "I won't. Now stop bothering me."

He turned away, muttering to himself. "I'll show them it's my pond," he thought, and he went off to gather an armful of sticks. He piled them by the pond and lit a fire.

"That will keep those annoyances away," he said, looking at the fire with satisfaction.

Zebra wasn't in the least scared by the fire. With a snort and a shake of his mane, he galloped to Baboon and kicked him hard.

Baboon shot up into the air. So did the sooty sticks from the fire... then both came tumbling down again.

The sticks landed on Zebra. Baboon landed on his bottom – smack in the middle of the fire. Ever since then, zebras have had black stripes and baboons have had red bottoms.

Dick Whittington

Country boy Dick Whittington was so poor that he decided to walk fifty miles to the city of London to seek his fortune. He'd heard the streets were paved with gold.

When he arrived, Dick discovered that the streets weren't golden at all, just dirty.

Exhausted after his long journey, Dick collapsed on the doorstep of a large house, just as a finely-dressed man came out.

"You look like you need a good meal, my boy," he said, kindly. "Come along inside."

The man was a rich merchant named Mr. Fitzwarren. He felt so sorry for Dick that he gave him a job in his kitchen. Dick worked hard all day, and that night was offered a bed in the attic.

He had just snuggled down when he heard a squeak... followed by another... and another...

Mice were popping up through the gaps in the floorboards. "I'll never sleep with this noise," he thought. Every night, the same thing happened.

On Friday, Mr. Fitzwarren gave Dick his first wages.

"Wow! A whole penny," said Dick excitedly. He knew just what to spend it on.

He visited the market and bought a cat. "You're sure to keep those noisy mice away," Dick told his new pet. "I'll call you Tom."

When the mice appeared as usual, Tom chased every single one back under the floorboards. Dick slept well at last.

A few days later, Mr. Fitzwarren called all his servants into his study. "One of my ships is going on a trading voyage," he announced. "If you have anything you want to sell, it can go on the ship today."

Now that the mice were gone, Dick decided to sell his cat. "Maybe someone will give me *two* whole pennies for him," he thought.

Dick couldn't sleep that night. He felt bad about selling Tom. What's more, the mice were back. "What have I done?" he sighed.

During the days that followed, Dick was so sleepy, he kept dropping plates on the kitchen floor. "Wake up, boy!" the cook yelled.

After a month of being shouted at, Dick had had enough. "I'm going back to the country," he thought.

Early the next morning, he sneaked out of the house and walked until he reached the edge of the city. Just then, the bells of a nearby church rang out. Dick was astonished. The bells sounded as if they were calling to him. *Turn again, Whittington*, they seemed to chime, *thrice mayor of London.*

"They're telling me to go back," Dick realized. "And they're saying I'll be mayor of London – three times! That's really strange."

Dick decided to take the bells' advice and hurried back to Mr. Fitzwarren's.

When he arrived, Dick found his old master waiting for him.

"Where have you been, lad?" he cried.

"I have great news for you."

Mr. Fitzwarren hurried Dick inside.
"The King of Barbary bought your cat," he
explained. "His palace was full of mice, and
Tom chased them all away."

Mr. Fitzwarren handed Dick two
bags bulging with gold
coins. "The King
sent you these as
payment," he said,
with a smile.

Dick used the gold to
buy and sell things, just
like Mr. Fitzwarren, and
he grew up to be one of
the richest men in the city.

Not only that, he became the most popular
mayor of London ever, three times, just as the
bells had said.

Jack and the Beanstalk

Jack and his mother were so poor that one day they ran out of food.

"You'll have to take the cow to market and sell her," Jack's mother said in despair. "Make sure you get a good price."

"Don't worry, of course I will," laughed Jack, looping some rope around the cow and setting off.

On the way, he passed an old man.

"Hello!" the man said. "Is the cow for sale?"

"For a good price she is," Jack replied.

"Well come closer," said the man. "I have just the thing," and he opened his hand to show Jack five dried beans.

"Old beans?" Jack said, doubtfully.

"These aren't any old beans," the man declared. "They're magic beans."

"Sold!" said Jack, at once, handing over the cow and taking the beans.

Back home, he showed them to his mother in delight.

She snatched them up and hurled them out of the window in disgust. "My son's a FOOL!" she raged, bursting into tears. "Believing nonsense like magic beans. Now we have nothing at all."

As Jack fell asleep that night, his tummy growled with hunger. The next morning, he was woken by huge leaves slapping against his window.

The beans had taken root and grown right up to the clouds.

In one minute, Jack was out of his window and climbing up the beanstalk, higher and higher until he reached the top. Ahead of him loomed an enormous castle. Jack started walking through the clouds to its vast wooden door.

Nervously, he jumped up and pulled at the bell rope, desperate for something to eat.

A giant woman opened the door. "Who's there?" she rumbled. Then she looked down. "A tiny boy!" she said.

"Please, do you have any food?" Jack asked.

"I do," she replied, "and you look harmless enough. Come on in and I'll feed you. But don't let my husband see you," she added. "He adores eating humans."

Jack had nearly finished his breakfast, when giant footsteps made the whole castle shake.

"HIDE!" screeched the giantess, popping Jack into a teapot, as the giant's chant echoed around the castle:

> *Fee fi fo fum, I smell the blood of a tasty man.*
> *Be he alive or be he dead*
> *I'll grind his bones to make my bread!*

"Calm down, dear," the giantess said, patting him. "There's no one here."

The giant sat down to his own breakfast, munching and belching.

"Bring my hen!" he yelled at his wife.

Lifting the teapot lid a crack, Jack watched the giantess set a hen on the table.

To Jack's astonishment, every time the giant said, "Lay!" the hen produced a shining golden egg.

Soon, the giant fell asleep, snoring so loudly that he shook the table.

"Now's my chance," Jack thought. He seized the hen, tore from the castle and slid back down the beanstalk.

"We're rich!" he crowed to his mother, who was amazed when she heard about the hen.

The two of them lived well for some time, selling the golden eggs whenever they needed more money.

But Jack thirsted for adventure. He couldn't resist climbing the beanstalk a second time and knocking at the castle door again. Before he went, he disguised himself so the giantess wouldn't recognize him.

"I'm not letting anyone in," she said. "Our last visitor stole my husband's hen."

"That's terrible!" said Jack, trying to sound sympathetic. "I would never do anything like that. Please, could you spare a morsel of supper? And then I'll go."

Just as before, Jack hid in the teapot when the giant burst in shouting, "Fee fi fo fum, I smell the blood of a tasty man."

"I don't think so," soothed the giantess. "Why don't you listen to your golden harp?"

Whenever the giant commanded, "Play," out came the most beautiful music, joyous at first, then gentle, until the giant was lulled to sleep.

"NOW," thought Jack, darting out, grabbing the harp and beginning his descent down the beanstalk.

"Master! Master!" wailed the harp, so mournfully that the giant woke.

"Thief!" he bellowed, following Jack as fast as he could.

By now, Jack had reached his garden. He grabbed a saw and hacked at the beanstalk with all his strength until the giant crashed to the ground – dead.

Jack and his mother lived happily ever after. As for the beanstalk, it withered away after being cut and, since no seeds had been gathered, it never grew again.

Brer Rabbit and the Tug of War

Brer Rabbit was bouncing up a hill, *lippety-loppety, lippety-loppety,* when he saw grumpy Old Rhino down in a dusty ditch.

Then, out of the corner of his eye, he spied Lady Hippo, wallowing in a patch of mud.

"Those two never show me any respect," tutted Brer Rabbit. "Wouldn't it be fun," he thought, whiskers twitching, "to play a trick on them…" And there, dangling from a branch above him, was just the thing to help – a twisty old vine.

"Wrinkly Rhino," he
called out. "I bet I could
beat you in a tug of war
contest. You wouldn't
stand a chance against
the mighty Brer Rabbit!"

Old Rhino laughed and laughed. "Of course
I could beat you, little pipsqueak," he cried.
"Give me that vine and I'll show you how
strong I am."

"If you're sure…" sang Brer Rabbit. "I'm
going around the hill. Wait until you feel me
pull my end of the vine. Then we'll begin."

Brer Rabbit bobbed off to Lady Hippo. "Do
you do anything but lie around in mud all day?
I bet I could beat you in a tug of war contest."

Lady Hippo spluttered in the mud. "How
dare you talk to me like that, you good-for-
nothing-ball-of-fluff! Give me that vine and I'll
show you how strong I am."

Brer Rabbit handed it over and bounded back the way he'd come. "Wait there!" he called. "When I pull my end, we'll begin."

When Brer Rabbit was halfway between the two great beasts, he twanged the vine.

Old Rhino and Lady Hippo both thought they were going to beat Brer Rabbit easily. They gave the vine a careless tug. Neither of them budged.

"Well this should do it," thought Old Rhino, and pulled with all his might.

"Whoah!" cried Lady Hippo, as she was dragged through the mud. "Heave-ho!" she hollered, straining back with a tremendous tug.

Old Rhino and Lady Hippo kept heaving
and pulling and tugging and groaning, until
their flanks shook and they were weak at
the knees.

Sitting on the hill, watching them both,
Brer Rabbit chuckled with delight. Then he
gnawed through the vine and
snapped it in two.

SPLASH! Lady Hippo
flew back in the mud.

SPLAT! Old Rhino
landed flat on his back.

When Lady Hippo
looked up, Brer Rabbit was
standing over her. "The vine
broke," he said. "Shall I find another?"

"No, no," said the panting hippo. "You're
stronger than me. How can that be?"

"I told you..." chanted Brer Rabbit, and
skipped off to Old Rhino.

"The vine broke," he said. "Here's a new one so we can start again."

"That's enough for me," puffed the rhino. "You're... a... mighty strong rabbit, you know."

From that day on, Lady Hippo and Old Rhino showed Brer Rabbit the greatest respect.

"Great Brer Rabbit!" they called, whenever he bobbed by. And Brer Rabbit would hold his head high and think, "Oh! How bold and brave and brilliant am I!"

Eros and Psyche

Psyche was the most beautiful girl the world had ever known. Everyone adored her, but nobody dared ask to marry her.

"She's too beautiful," they whispered.

This made Aphrodite, the goddess of love, extremely jealous. "No human can be worshipped like a goddess," she raged.

She ordered her son, Eros, to fire one of his magic arrows and make Psyche fall in love with the ugliest person in her village.

Eros flew at once in search of Psyche, expecting to find a vain, proud human. Instead he saw a charming, carefree girl and fell in love with her himself.

He watched Psyche from a distance and noticed her parents watching too. "I can't understand why no one will marry our Psyche," sighed her father. "Maybe we should ask the gods what to do."

"Here's my chance," thought Eros. In a low voice he called out, "Send her alone to the nearest mountain top. The wind will take her to the husband of her dreams."

Psyche's parents knew it was foolish to disobey the gods, so the next morning they waved a tearful goodbye and watched their daughter climb the steep mountain path. There, the West Wind gently blew her off the rocky ground and swept her far away.

Psyche floated on the Wind until he
set her down in a sweet-scented valley.
A golden palace stood before her
and, as she approached it, the doors
swung open. She heard and saw no one, but
everything seemed prepared for her arrival.
Freshly-made meals appeared on the table
and in the evening lamps were mysteriously
lit. They guided Psyche to her bedroom,
waited for her to slip under the downy cover
on the bed, then blew themselves out.

Alone in the dark, Psyche wondered when
her husband would appear.

"I'm here now," came a low voice. It was
filled with such tenderness that Psyche wasn't
at all afraid.

"Was it you who made those delicious
meals?" she asked.

"Yes," replied the voice. "I hope you'll be
happy here."

"Very," murmured Psyche. She reached across the bed, found her husband's warm hand and held it as she fell asleep.

The next morning, there was no sign of a soul, but Psyche felt at ease in her new home. Evening came and she eagerly blew out the lamp, hoping that her husband would return.

And he did.

They talked until the small hours, blissfully content in each other's company, but when the sun rose, Psyche awoke alone.

This strange pattern continued day after day. Psyche had never felt happier, though she wondered how her parents were without her.

"I'd like to visit my family," she told her husband one night, "just to let them know that I'm alive and well."

"Please don't," he begged. "They will be suspicious and ask why you never see me. But if you discover who I am, I'll have to leave."

"I love you," was Psyche's reply, "and I trust you."

So her husband arranged for the West Wind to carry Psyche to her family. Psyche's parents were delighted to see their daughter looking so radiant. Her sisters were less accepting and pestered her with questions.

"Your husband won't let you see him?" they scoffed. "He must be an ugly monster!"

Psyche shook her head. "He's kind, gentle and loving," she replied.

"Then why won't he let you see him? Take a peek when he's asleep – he'll never know."

When Psyche returned to her husband, she couldn't forget her sisters' words. That night, curiosity got the better of her and as her husband slept she quietly lit a lamp. The face it illuminated took her breath away. It belonged to none other than Eros, the god of love.

In her surprise,
Psyche let a drop
of oil fall from
her lamp onto
his chest. Eros
awoke with a
start and stared in
horror at his wife.

"You've ruined everything!"
he cried, and raced out of the door.

Psyche was miserable with regret. She
searched in vain for Eros and eventually
found herself in a temple in front of a statue
of Aphrodite. "Please help me find Eros," she
prayed. "We love each other so much."

Aphrodite was aghast to discover that her
son had been living with this human. She
decided to punish them both.

"First, you must prove to me how much
you love him," she commanded.

Aphrodite set Psyche one challenge after another. Fearless in her love, Psyche attempted each one. First, she had to separate a mound of mixed-up grain, but the ants took pity on her and helped. Then she had to gather golden fleeces but the grass felt sorry for her and, in a whisper, told her what to do.

The final task was to retrieve Persephone's box of everlasting beauty. Persephone was the Queen of the Underworld and only the dead could enter her forbidding kingdom. Psyche was preparing to throw herself off a tall tower, when the tower itself took pity on her.

"You don't have to kill yourself," it said. "Just step off the cliff over there and you'll be at the river leading to the Underworld. Pay Charon the ferryman to take you across, and throw honeyed bread to Cerberus, the monstrous dog who guards the entrance."

Clutching some coins and bread, Psyche stepped boldly off the cliff and found herself in a tunnel by an underground river. With payment for the old ferryman and sweet treats to distract the dog, she arrived unscathed at Queen Persephone's throne.

"You are brave beyond measure," said the Queen. "You may take my box."

"Thank you, your highness," said Psyche. She couldn't believe her luck as she raced back to the world of the living. Then doubt crept in.

"I am no match for a god," she murmured, looking at the box she was holding. "But maybe with a sprinkling of Persephone's everlasting beauty..."

She carefully lifted the lid.

Alas, instead of everlasting beauty, the box contained everlasting sleep and she sank into slumber. At once, Eros was by her side, blowing the sleep from her eyes. In angry defiance of his mother, he whisked Psyche through the clouds to Mount Olympus, to stand before Zeus, the king of the gods.

"Please help us," Eros said with urgency. "Psyche and I are in love, but my mother won't agree to our marriage since Psyche is only human..."

Zeus appeared amused by Eros' plight. "No human deserves to be this beautiful," he remarked. "Perhaps making her immortal will solve the problem."

The powerful god touched Psyche lightly on her head and she felt her whole being transformed. Eros gazed adoringly at his immortal wife. "My true love," he said. "We need never live in secret or be parted again."

The Mouse's Wedding

There was once a proud father mouse, who lived in a snug home beside a mountain, with his wife and their beloved daughter.

"Look how grown-up our daughter has become," said the wife one day. "It's time we found her a suitable husband."

The father mouse agreed. "We will find her the best, most powerful husband in the whole world," he said, lovingly.

The following morning, all three set off on the search. At length, the father mouse said, "Aha! There is the best husband for you."

Curious, his daughter looked around.

Her father pointed up to the Sun.

"Isn't he the strongest, most powerful husband you could ever imagine?"

The young mouse looked at the Sun, then at her father. "He's far too hot," she stated. "Please find me someone else."

"O Sun," asked the father mouse. "Is there anyone more powerful than you?"

"Indeed there is," said the Sun. "The Cloud can cover my face and block out all my light and warmth." And even as he spoke, a cloud scudded across the sky.

"I see," replied the father mouse. "Then daughter, why don't you marry the Cloud?"

"Oh no I couldn't," said the young mouse. "He's far too dark and cold. Please find me a better husband."

Eager to please his daughter, the father mouse addressed the Cloud. "Please tell me, O Cloud, is there anyone more powerful than you?"

"Indeed there is," said the Cloud. "One puff from the Wind and I'm driven far across the sky."

"That's true," thought the father mouse. He turned to his daughter. "The Wind is mightier still. You may marry him."

"Father!" she replied indignantly. "He just comes and goes as he pleases. I want a reliable husband."

"Of course," the father agreed. "O Wind," he called respectfully. "Is there anyone more powerful than you?"

"Indeed there is," said the Wind, "The Mountain, for however strong I blow, he always remains unmoved."

The father clapped his hands. "That's it!" he cried. "You can marry the Mountain."

"Father!" groaned the young mouse. "He's boring. Please choose me someone else."

"Dear me," murmured the father, "this is trickier than I thought... O Mountain," he called out. "I don't suppose there's anyone more powerful than you?"

"Indeed there is," said the Mountain. "There's a young mouse burrowing under my lower slope and there's nothing I can do to stop him."

"A *mouse*?" said the father in surprise.

"A mouse!" squealed his daughter in delight.

Just then, a handsome young mouse popped his head out from a tunnel in the mountainside. Seeing him, the daughter's eyes twinkled.

"Would you like this *mouse* to be your husband?" asked her mother.

The daughter nodded.

"Well, I suppose he is more powerful than anyone else in the world..." said her father.

So the two mice were married the following month, and an extra special guest came to their wedding: the Sun.

Anansi and the Bag of Wisdom

This is the story of how wisdom came to the world and it starts with a spider...

Anansi was king of the spiders. He lived deep in Africa, among haughty giraffes, friendly zebras and chattering monkeys.

One afternoon, as he basked in the sun, the sky god appeared before him.

"Anansi," said the god, "I have a very important job for you."

"Something only a king can do, I expect," Anansi said, nodding.

The god held out a patterned bag. "This bag contains all the wisdom in the world."

"All of it?" said Anansi, in excitement.

"Every last scrap," said the god. "I'm giving it to you, but I want you to spread it around. Promise me you'll share it."

"If you want…" Anansi said, carelessly.

As soon as the god had left, he looked in the bag. It was bursting with brilliant ideas. Anansi frowned. He didn't see why he should share the wisdom with the giraffes, the zebras and the monkeys, or the humans he sometimes saw.

"I'm going to keep it all to myself," he decided. "I'll be the cleverest creature in the world and even the sky god won't be able to outwit me. I'd better hide the bag."

Clutching it tightly, he scurried off to the tallest tree he could see.

Then he hooked the bag around his neck so it hung down his front.

Anansi's son had seen the god give his father the bag, and followed him.

"What are you doing, Dad?" he asked.

"Oh, just putting this old bag in the tree out of the way," Anansi replied, with a shrug.

He began to climb the trunk but the bag banged against his middle and he kept losing his hold on the tree and falling to the ground.

After watching his father fall off for the fourth time, his son made a suggestion.

"Why don't you put the bag on your back?" he said. "It won't get in the way and you'll be able to climb the tree."

Anansi twisted the bag around, so it was on his back, and tried again. His son was right.

He scuttled up the tree in no
time, but he wasn't happy.
He was outraged.

"How did you know I needed to put
the bag on my back?" he shouted to his
son. "I'm the one with the bag of wisdom.
I should have known the answer for myself."

With a scowl, he ripped the bag from his
back and threw it from the tree.

The bag went plummeting to the ground
and burst open.

Wisdom flew out, curling up into the air,
and floated away on the warm
breezes. It reached into every
corner of the world.

And that is why,
today, everyone
knows something...
but no one knows
everything.

The Musicians of Bremen

There was once a donkey who had worked hard all his life. He carried heavy sacks for his master without ever grumbling, but he was getting old.

"He's no use to me now," thought the master. "I won't waste any more food on him."

When the donkey caught wind of the master's plan, he escaped and set off down the road to Bremen.

"I'll become a musician," he decided. "That seems a good life for an old donkey."

On his way he met a hunting dog, panting heavily by the side of the road.

"Where have you run from and where are you going?" asked the donkey.

"I've run away from my master," replied the dog. "He wanted to shoot me because I'm too old to hunt. So I escaped, but now I have nowhere to go."

"Then come with me," suggested the donkey. "I'm going to be a musician in Bremen. You could play the drums while I play the lute."

The dog liked the sound of this, and walked alongside the donkey. They hadn't gone far when they met an annoyed, bedraggled cat.

"What *is* the matter?" asked the donkey.

"My mistress tried to drown me," spat the cat. "I've grown too old to chase mice and she won't let me just curl up by the stove."

"Then come with us!" said the dog.

"We're going to be musicians in Bremen," the donkey explained. "You can play the violin."

The cat loved this idea, and padded alongside them. It was getting dark as they neared a farm. Perched on the gate was a rooster, crowing at the top of his voice.

"Whatever's wrong?" asked the donkey.

"My mistress has decided my time is up," sighed the rooster. "She's going to chop off my head and cook me for Sunday lunch."

"Don't let her," said the donkey. "Come with us."

"We're going to be musicians in Bremen," said the dog.

"You can be our singer!" added the cat.

So the four animals walked on until they reached a forest, where they settled for the night by a tall pine tree.

"I'm cold," moaned the cat.

"I'm hungry," moaned the dog.

"Hang on," called the rooster, "I see a light."

The animals followed the light and found a snug little cottage. The donkey crept closer and peered in at the window.

"I see a table of food!" he said with excitement. "And a band of robbers," he added in dismay.

Whispering in the shadows, the animals came up with a plan. Quietly, the dog climbed on the donkey, the cat jumped on the dog, the rooster flew onto the cat and, with a blast of song, they burst through the window.

"Run for your lives!" the robbers cried, leaving the animals to enjoy their feast.

Happy and full, the animals turned out the light and lay down to sleep.

But the robbers hadn't gone far. When he saw the light go out, the robber captain called the youngest robber. "Go back and find out who stole our hideout," he ordered.

All was still as the little robber tiptoed into the dark kitchen. He saw the cat's eyes gleaming and, thinking they were burning coals, jabbed a candle at them to light it.

"Aiiieeekk!" squealed the cat, leaping up and scratching the robber.

Terrified, he ran to the back door and tripped over the dog, who bit him savagely on the leg.

The robber hobbled into the yard and was bucked by the donkey, while the rooster crowed a fearsome COCK-A-DOODLE-DOO!

Scared out of his mind, the robber escaped into the forest. "We must run away!" he told his captain. "I've just been scratched by a witch, stabbed by a thug and beaten by a monster, and now an evil voice is yelling, 'Catch that rascal, do!'"

The band of robbers turned and fled and never returned to the cottage in the woods. As for the animal musicians, they liked their new home so much, they decided to stay and never did get to Bremen after all.

King Thrushbeard

The King was getting desperate. It was time for his only daughter, Milly, to get married and she had refused every prince he had suggested. She did 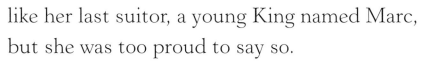 like her last suitor, a young King named Marc, but she was too proud to say so.

"Your pointed beard looks like a thrush's beak," she mocked, and from then on, everyone called him King Thrushbeard.

Her father lost patience. "Since you insist on being so proud and rude, you shall marry the first man to come to the palace tomorrow!"

The next morning, a beggar arrived at the palace gates, playing a battered old violin.

"Have him enter," ordered the King.

"Would you like a tune, your Majesty?" the beggar said, and a haunting melody filled the throne room.

"Very lovely," said the King. "But I asked you in because my daughter is looking for a husband. Would you like to marry her?"

The beggar looked at Milly, who sneered at him. "How is she at chores?" he asked.

"Chores?" shrieked Milly.

"Oh, she's a quick learner," the King said.

"Well, beggars can't be choosers," said the beggar with a wink, "and I do need a wife..."

Milly looked horrified. "He's a commoner!" she spat. "I can't marry a commoner."

"But you didn't like any of the princes I found," her father pointed out, and the couple were married on the spot.

The journey to the beggar's house took days. They walked through forests and fields, past bustling towns and a magnificent castle.

"Whose kingdom is this?" Milly wondered.

"King Thrushbeard's," replied the beggar.

"*King Thrushbeard*?" thought Milly. She sighed. All this could have been hers.

"Cheer up!" said the beggar, seeing her glum face. "We're nearly there."

By now, they were in a village. He strode up to a ramshackle hut. "Welcome home!"

Milly burst into tears.

The beggar looked worried. "Don't cry," he said. "It's basic, but it has all we need."

And so Milly's new life began. The beggar was kind and caring but he was desperately poor. As a princess, Milly had servants to do everything for her. Married to the beggar, she had to do everything herself. She had no time to be haughty, she was simply too busy.

The beggar set off each day to earn a few pennies, leaving Milly with the chores.

At first, she was hopeless, but the beggar was patient with her mistakes, and so caring that she grew fond of him.

One day, he came home without a single penny, and no food. "We need to earn more money somehow," he sighed.

Milly nodded, hunger gnawing at her.

The day after that, the beggar came home with news. "King Thrushbeard is getting married!" he said. "They need an extra kitchen maid up at the castle."

"A maid?" thought Milly, but she could see that she had no choice, and set out for the castle kitchen the very next morning.

"I can't wait to hear all about it," the beggar said, his eyes twinkling as he waved her off.

Milly had never worked so hard. When the wedding feast was finally ready, the cook filled Milly's pockets with titbits, and let her go to the throne room to watch the festivities.

Milly was grubby after her morning's work, so she hid behind a curtain.

King Thrushbeard was welcoming his guests. Milly peeped out for a better look.

"He's handsome!" she thought.

To her surprise, he smiled at her and walked over. "Would you like to dance?" he asked.

"Me?" said Milly. "But I look a mess."

"Come on," he said, taking her hand.

Milly felt the guests staring at her. She pulled away and food fell from her pockets, sending a ripple of laughter around the room.

"Ignore them," said the King in a softer voice, a twinkle in his eyes.

Milly was astonished. "You look exactly like my husband. You sound like him too."

King Thrushbeard smiled again. "I am your husband. I fell in love with you when we first met, but you were so proud, I knew you wouldn't say, even if you liked me too."

"I did like you," Milly admitted. "I do."

"I heard your father tell you to marry the first man to come to the palace, so I disguised myself as a beggar to teach you a lesson. Do you forgive me?"

Milly blushed as she thought of how horrible she'd been. "Of course I forgive you," she said.

"Thank goodness for that," said the King.

Milly was whisked away, cleaned up and dressed in a rose pink gown.

As she returned to the throne room, King Thrushbeard announced, "Meet your new Queen!" and all the guests cheered.

"Thank you," Milly whispered to him. "I know now it doesn't matter what people look like, or who they are. I'd be happy if you were still a beggar – but I'm very glad you're a King!"

Pandora's Box

Many moons ago, in the world of Ancient Greece, only the gods knew the secret of fire. Prometheus, one of their relatives, thought this very unfair. He saw humans shivering in the cold and living off raw food and decided to share the secret.

When Zeus, king of the gods, found out, he was furious and stormed into Prometheus' home. "How dare you give fire to the humans?" he bellowed.

Prometheus was unapologetic. "They deserved to know! And you didn't even notice. You were too busy partying."

"That does it!" Zeus fumed, dragging Prometheus to a mountainside and chaining him to a rocky ledge. "Here you must endure your punishment, until you are truly sorry."

The punishment was horrific. Every day, Zeus would send a giant eagle to peck out Prometheus' liver. Because Prometheus was immortal, the liver grew again overnight, only to be pecked out once more the following day. Even then, Prometheus didn't regret his action.

Zeus wasn't satisfied and turned his anger to the humans. "They should never have accepted a stolen gift," he said to the other gods. "They shall be punished, not by us but by one of their own kind."

The gods set about sculpting a woman out of clay. Aphrodite, goddess of love, showered her with beauty. Athena, goddess of weaving, spun her an elegant gown, and Hermes, the messenger god, hid a bundle of curiosity in her heart. Then all the gods breathed life into her and her eyes flickered open.

"You are Pandora," Zeus announced, "and will marry Epimetheus, Prometheus' brother.

My wedding present to you is this priceless box. But whatever you do, *don't* open it."

With that, Hermes flew her to Epimetheus' house. Pandora and Epimetheus fell in love on the spot and were married.

"What's that box you keep looking at?" asked Epimetheus, one evening.

"It's a wedding gift from Zeus," replied Pandora, "only he said not to open it."

"Then you must obey him," warned Epimetheus.

Pandora nodded, but she was prickling with curiosity. "Why shouldn't I open it?" she thought to herself. "What harm can it do? I could lift the lid a tiny bit and just quickly peek inside..."

She waited until Epimetheus was out, then gingerly picked up the box. Her fingers curled around the lid and gently she lifted it.

SCRRRRRAAAAAAAARRRKK!

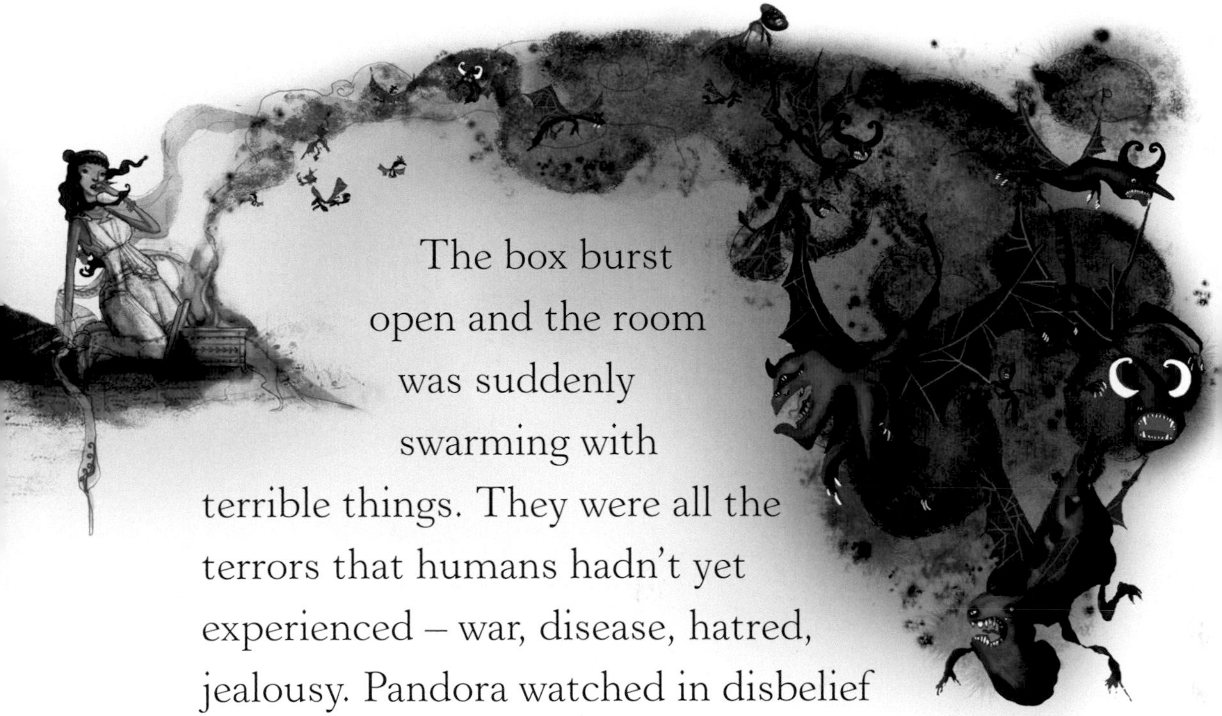

The box burst
open and the room
was suddenly
swarming with
terrible things. They were all the
terrors that humans hadn't yet
experienced – war, disease, hatred,
jealousy. Pandora watched in disbelief
as they escaped into the air and spread
across the world. She hung her head in shame,
before noticing one last thing flutter out like a
beautiful dragonfly.

It was hope.

The Reluctant Dragon

Harold's dad rushed into the house. "You won't believe it," he panted. "Th... th... there's a dragon up in the hills!"

Harold gasped. He'd never seen a dragon before. "What was it like?" he asked eagerly. "Did it breathe fire? How tall was it?"

"All I know is it was huge and horrible," replied his father, still trembling. "I didn't stay around to measure it."

Harold decided to go and look himself. The next day, he set off up the hill. Spotting a puff of smoke in the distance, he followed it until he reached a cave. Sitting casually outside was a big, green dragon, who didn't look scary in the least.

"Hello!" said Harold.

"Ah, a friendly face at last," said the dragon. "I've been getting very lonely up here."

Harold spent all day chatting with his new friend. The dragon told him stories of long ago, when fire-breathing dragons terrorized the land. Back then, brave knights battled dragons to keep the locals safe.

"But I'm not interested in fighting," said the dragon. "I like a quiet life."

Harold couldn't wait to tell everyone about the dragon. But he soon wished he hadn't.

When the villagers heard there was a dragon nearby, they went crazy.

"We'll be burned in our beds!" they cried. "Someone call for a dragon slayer."

Soon afterwards, George the Dragon Killer rode into the village, brandishing his spear.

"I hear you need my help," the knight said to Harold. "Someone told me there's a dangerous fire-breathing dragon up in the hills."

"He's not dangerous," said Harold. "In fact, he's not in the least interested in fighting anyone."

Harold led George to the dragon's cave.

"What a perfect spot for a fight," George said, as the dragon lumbered towards them.

"But I don't want to fight," wailed the dragon. He frowned at George.

"Those villagers won't leave you in peace until we do," said George, polishing his spear.

"I have an idea," said Harold, with a grin.

He told George and the dragon his plan, then ran down to the village.

"George will fight the dragon tomorrow!" he announced in a loud voice.

The villagers cheered.

"And when the dragon's dead, we'll have a feast to celebrate," they declared.

The next morning, a huge crowd gathered outside the dragon's cave.

There was a deafening roar, and the dragon burst out, flames pouring from his nostrils.

The crowd trembled.

"Never fear, George is here!" cried the knight, galloping straight for the dragon on his trusty horse.

George's spear missed the dragon by a whisker. He turned and charged again. This time, the pair collided in a cloud of dust. There were screams and shouts, but no one could see what was actually happening. Finally, the dust settled and George stood victorious.

"The dragon is beaten," he yelled.

"Let's kill it!" shouted one of the villagers.

"No," said George firmly. "I think he's
learned his lesson," he added, giving Harold
a sly wink. The boy's plan only to pretend to
fight had worked.

So the villagers agreed to let the dragon
live. They even invited him to join in
their celebrations.

"Hop up," the dragon said to Harold, and
he gave him a ride, as he followed the villagers
marching off to enjoy a glorious feast.

The Roly-Poly Rice Ball

Long ago, in Japan, there lived a poor woodcutter named Miki. He was so poor, he could hardly afford any food. One morning, all he had left was a handful of rice.

"I'll save it for later," he decided. So he rolled it into a ball, wrapped it up and set off into the forest.

Miki chopped wood all morning. By lunchtime, he was starving. He was just unwrapping the rice ball when...

"Oh no!"

It slipped from his fingers.

Before he could stop
it, the rice ball had
rolled into a hole.
Miki reached after
it, stumbled – and
tumbled in too.

He slid down in the
dark and landed with a
bump! Miki looked up and
blinked in astonishment. He was in a cave lit
by tiny lanterns, and full of mice, who were
singing and dancing around him.

"A roly-poly rice ball, a roly-poly treat," they
sang. "Roll away, roll away, here for us to eat."

In a corner, more mice were turning the rice
ball into tiny, mouse-sized cakes. "Come and
join our feast,"
they squeaked.
"Thank you!"
Miki smiled.

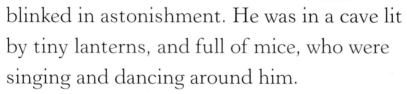

Soon, he was eating, singing and dancing along. Finally, feeling full and exhausted, he realized it was time to go.

"Thank you for the rice," squeaked the mice, as they said goodbye. "In return, we have a gift for you." And they handed Miki a tiny golden spoon.

Miki waved the spoon. Gold coins rained down. "Wow!" He waved it again, and a bowl of steaming rice appeared. "I'll never be poor or hungry again," he gasped. "Thank you!"

Goldilocks and the Three Bears

The Three Bears – great big Father Bear, middle-sized Mother Bear and tiny Baby Bear – lived quietly in their cottage in the middle of the woods.

One morning, they went for a walk before breakfast, leaving the door unlocked because they didn't expect a visitor at such an early hour. This was a big mistake, as you will see.

That very day, Goldilocks was exploring the woods. She was an inquisitive, naughty little girl, with bright golden curls all over her head.

"What a lovely cottage," smiled Goldilocks.

Bear Cottage

She pushed the door open and saw three bowls of porridge laid on the table.

"Mmm," she murmured hungrily, taking a spoonful from the biggest bowl. It was so hot, she spat it straight out. Next, she tried the middle-sized bowl, but that was too cold. Finally, she tried the porridge in the tiny bowl and that was so delicious, she ate it all up.

Feeling full, she decided to sit down. First, she tried the biggest chair, but the cushion was too hard. Then she settled in the middle-sized one, but that was too soft. At last, she jumped into the tiny chair. It was exactly right, but she landed so hard that it broke into pieces.

"Oops!" said Goldilocks, giggling, and she decided to go upstairs. There was only one bedroom, with three different-sized beds.

Each bed was made up with smooth, clean sheets and looked inviting. Goldilocks leaped into the biggest, but it was uncomfortably high. Then she tried the middle-sized bed. "Too low," she decided, kicking off the sheets, "but I'm sure the tiny one will be perfect."

She snuggled down and fell fast asleep. She slept so soundly, she didn't hear the three bears coming back.

"Someone's been tasting MY porridge," roared Father Bear.

"And mine," wailed Mother Bear, while Baby Bear, staring sadly at his empty bowl, squeaked, "Someone's been tasting MY

porridge and they've eaten it ALL up!"

Next they saw the chairs.

"Someone's been sitting in MY chair," bellowed Father Bear.

"Someone's been sitting in my chair," cried Mother Bear.

Baby Bear just howled. "Someone's been sitting in MY chair," he sobbed, "and now it's all broken."

They raced upstairs to their bedroom and found rumpled sheets all over the floor.

"Someone's been sleeping in MY bed," growled Father Bear.

"Someone's been sleeping in my bed," shuddered Mother Bear.

"Someone's been sleeping in MY bed – and here she is!" screamed Baby Bear.

Goldilocks woke with a start, feeling the bears' breath hot on her face; their growls, shudders and screams echoing in her ears.

She jumped out of bed, ran down the stairs and tore out of the door, never stopping till she was safe in her own home.

The Three Bears never saw her again. But whether she was cured of being inquisitive – or naughty – nobody knows.

Clever Rabbit and the Wolves

Clever Rabbit was busy eating grass. So busy, he forgot to look out for danger... until he saw a large wolf-shaped shadow looming over him. He looked to the left — could he escape that way? No, there was a greedy-looking wolf, waiting for him. He looked to the right, only to see another wolf, drooling at the sight of him.

He spun around. His worst fears were confirmed — he was smack in the middle of a ring of wolves.

"Dinner time," said the Chief Wolf, licking his lips.

"Wait!" cried Clever Rabbit.

"What for?" asked the Chief Wolf, coming closer, sharp teeth gleaming, red tongue lolling.

Clever Rabbit wasn't sure. But he had to think of something before he was munched. "My dance!" he cried. "You've never seen it."

"But I don't *want* to see your dance," snarled the Chief Wolf.

"I'd like to," said the littlest wolf.

Clever Rabbit began to tap his foot. "*La, la, la,*" he sang. "Copy me everyone."

All the wolves began tapping their feet. "*La, la, la,*" they sang in their snarly growly voices.

"What now?" asked the littlest wolf.

"*La, la, la. Tum-ti-tum,*" sang Clever Rabbit. "Turn around on the word *tum.*"

The wolves began turning around.

"This is easy," said the Chief Wolf. He put his paws on his hips. He licked his lips again.

"Try it faster," said Clever Rabbit, spinning around. *"La, la, la. Tum-ti-tum tum,"* he sang, faster and faster.

The wolves spun around in a whirl of fur. They stumbled and tripped and fell in a heap, dizzy and wobbling and dazed.

Clever Rabbit kept singing, but as he sang, he crept further and further away.

"Where's that rabbit?" asked the Chief Wolf.

"He's gone!" cried the littlest wolf. "He just disappeared, over that hill."

And the wolves were too dizzy to chase him.

The Greedy Dog

Dog was always hungry. He dreamed of sizzling bacon, succulent sausages and steaming steak pies. He also dreamed of catching birds and rabbits although, in real life, they always got away.

One day, he was sniffing around the market, when he saw a big, juicy bone, in a basket beneath the butcher's stall. No one was looking. So he jumped up, grabbed the bone in his jaws, and raced away through a forest of legs. No one had spotted him.

Dog was feeling very, very pleased with himself. He wagged his tail with glee. He was the cleverest dog in town! He raced past the shops, out into the countryside through the cornfields, and only stopped when he came to a river.

As he looked down into the water, he started, and almost yelped. There, in the water, was another dog, with an even bigger bone between his teeth.

"It's not fair!" Dog thought to himself. "His bone is bigger than mine."

He growled. The dog in the river growled back. He snarled. The dog in the river snarled back. He barked – and the bone dropped from his mouth. It fell in the river with a splash.

Seeing his bone floating away, Dog dived in after it. It was only then, with the cold water around his ears, and the bone nowhere in sight, that he realized something. There had never been another bone. The other dog had just been his reflection.

Panting and barking, Dog eventually made it to the riverbank, pulled himself out of the water, and shook himself dry.

If he had been hungry before, now he was ravenous. He walked all the way back to town feeling sorry for himself – and very, very foolish indeed.

Androcles and the Lion

Mop, scrub, dust, clean. Poor Androcles had a life of back-breaking drudgery. He was sick and tired of slaving for lazy Grossus in his big, fancy house near Rome.

When Androcles wasn't cleaning, he was cooking. He never had a moment's rest...

...and all he got for his work was one hard, little lump of cheese a day.

So Androcles decided to escape. He tip-toed out of the house at midnight and ran into the forest nearby.

The moon cast spooky
shadows through the
branches and Androcles
felt a shiver run up his
spine. He hadn't gone
far, when he heard a
creepy howl.

"Ooooowwww!"

It sounded like some terrible monster, and
it was coming from behind a bush.

Taking a deep breath, Androcles sneaked
up to the bush, and came face to face with...

...an enormous lion.

"Aagh!" screamed Androcles, but before he
could run, the lion spoke.

"Please help me!" he moaned. "There's a
thorn in my paw and I can't get it out."

"Um, okay," said Androcles nervously. He
took hold of the lion's paw and pulled out the
thorn, as gently as he could.

"Ooo, that's better," sighed the lion. "Thanks. My name's Leo, by the way."

From that day on, Androcles and Leo lived together in the forest and became best friends.

One morning, Androcles was collecting berries when a soldier leaped out at him.

"Gotcha!" cried the soldier. "You must be the escaped slave I've been looking for."

He threw Androcles into a cart and they trundled all the way to Rome, where the cart stopped in front of an enormous round building. A fat guard named Nickus was there to meet them.

"Welcome to the arena, skinny!" said Nickus with a chuckle. He dragged Androcles from the cart and bundled him inside.

Nickus marched Androcles down a long, dark corridor until they reached a dingy prison cell.

"What happens now?" asked Androcles.

"Tomorrow, you'll go into the arena to fight," explained Nickus.

"Fight? Fight who?" asked Androcles with a shudder.

Nickus laughed. "Why, the ferocious man-eating lions of course!"

Androcles didn't get much sleep that night.

The next morning, he was taken from his cell and pushed into the arena. All around sat thousands of rowdy, noisy Romans. "Bring on the lion!" they yelled.

Suddenly, a door opened and a massive, slobbering lion charged out.

"Oh no!" howled Androcles, falling to his knees. "I'll be eaten alive."

But, instead of fighting him, the lion gave Androcles a friendly lick.

"Leo!" cried Androcles, recognizing his old friend. "How did you get here?"

"I was captured just after you," explained Leo. "They brought me here and stuck me in a cage with lots of other lions."

The crowd couldn't believe their eyes. "Androcles has tamed the lion," they yelled. "What a hero! Hooray for Androcles!"

The Roman Emperor was so impressed, he let Androcles and the lion go. And so the pair ran back to their forest home – safe, happy and free.

The Stonecutter

In Japan, a long time ago, there lived a humble stonecutter. Every day, he chipped away at the side of a great mountain, making bricks and gravestones.

One afternoon, he delivered some bricks to the house of a wealthy man. The stonecutter had never seen such a vast mansion. He peeked into the bedroom and gasped in awe at the enormous bed, with its silk curtains and golden tassels.

"I wish I was rich enough to have a bed like that," he sighed to himself, "then I wouldn't have to sweat away all day, cutting stone."

Suddenly, a voice came from nowhere.

"A rich man you shall be," it said.

The stonecutter couldn't see a soul. But he'd heard of a mountain spirit who granted poor men's wishes. Perhaps it was him.

When he went home, the stonecutter was amazed to find that his little wooden hut had been replaced with a magnificent palace full of servants. So he gave up his job and lived a life of luxury.

He was walking in the grounds of his new home when he noticed that the sun had scorched the grass on his lawn.

"The sun is so much mightier than me," he grumbled. "I wish I was the sun."

"The sun you shall be," said a familiar voice.

And so the stonecutter became the sun. He spent his time blazing down on the ground below, warming the world and making flowers grow.

He might have stayed happy as the sun, but
then a cloud floated along and covered his face.
"This cloud is stopping me from shining,"
he moaned. "It's even more powerful
than me. I wish I was a cloud."
"A cloud you shall be," said the spirit.
So the stonecutter became a cloud.
He rained down on the land, filling
the rivers and lakes, and making
the grass a rich velvety green.
He was soon carried away
with his new power. He poured rain on the
Earth until the rivers overflowed and the fields
flooded. Only the mountains were safe from
his floods.

"I wish I was a mountain," he thought
to himself.

"A mountain you shall be," said the spirit.
The stonecutter was transformed into a
massive mountain. He felt strong and powerful.

Then along came a stonecutter, who began chipping away at him.

"Hey!" he yelled. "That man can knock chunks off me and I can't do a thing to stop him. If only I were a man."

The spirit's voice wafted down to him. "A man once more you shall be."

And so the stonecutter was his old self again. He went back to his job, making bricks and gravestones. It was hard work, but he didn't mind, for he had learned to be happy with his life.

Ali Baba and the Forty Thieves

Once upon a time, in a city in Persia, there lived two brothers. Cassim was a rich merchant, but Ali Baba was only a poor woodcutter. One day, Ali Baba was chopping wood in the forest when a band of forty thieves, led by their captain, Gamal, galloped past carrying bags bulging with gold.

Ali Baba hid behind a tree and watched, as Gamal walked up to a slab of rock and cried, "Open Sesame!" Ali Baba blinked in surprise, for a secret door groaned open in the rock and the thieves dashed in with their gold.

When they came out again, empty-handed, Gamal called, "Shut Sesame!" the rock slid back, and they all rode away.

"Amazing," thought Ali Baba, and he tried shouting, "Open Sesame!" just as Gamal had done. Once more, the door in the rock swung open, to reveal a cave filled with treasure.

"Surely, they won't miss a little gold," Ali Baba muttered, scooping up as many bags as he could carry. After he'd cried, "Shut Sesame!" he raced back to the city.

His wife was thrilled to see the gold. She was ready to go to the market at once.

Ali Baba stopped her. "We can't spend it right away," he pointed out. "People would wonder where it came from, and if the thieves ever found out I took it..."

"We could at least see how much we have," said his wife and she went to visit Cassim, to borrow his scales.

"Why do you need our scales?" demanded Cassim's wife.

"Oh... to weigh grain," Ali Baba's wife replied. She tried to look innocent, but Cassim's wife was suspicious.

"Ali Baba is poor," she said to herself. "He would never have enough grain to measure." Secretly, she greased the scales all over with butter. "There," she muttered. "Whatever Ali Baba weighs will stick."

Sure enough, when Ali Baba's wife returned the scales, Cassim's wife found a gold coin stuck underneath. Triumphantly, she sent Cassim to question his brother.

Ali Baba couldn't lie, so he told Cassim about the cave and the password.

Cassim's eyes lit up with greed.

The next day, he drove ten donkeys laden with ten saddlebags to the rock, opened it and went inside, closing the rock behind him.

Cassim was entranced by the treasures in the cave. He gently packed up luxurious silks and seized strings of pearls and ropes of rubies. He grabbed amethysts, sapphires and fistfuls of diamonds, plundering every chest until his saddlebags were bursting.

When he came to leave, he had completely forgotten the words to move the stone.

"Open up!" he shouted, but of course the stone didn't move. "Open barley!" he cried in desperation. "Open corn! Open chickpea!"

Nothing worked. Poor Cassim was stuck there until the thieves came back. When they saw him, they killed him on the spot.

Cassim's wife was so worried when he didn't return that she asked Ali Baba for help. He searched everywhere for Cassim without success, until he tried the cave, where he found his brother's body. Beside himself with grief, he carried it home.

"No one must know how he died," Ali Baba told Cassim's widow. "If the thieves hear, they'll know we discovered the secret of their cave and they'll come after us."

Together with Cassim's clever servant, Morgiana, he came up with a plan.

That day, Morgiana went to buy medicine in the market, telling everyone she spoke to that Cassim was sick.

Over the next few days, she said he was getting worse. At last, she announced that he had died. Finally, he could be buried.

After the funeral, Cassim's widow invited Ali Baba and his family to move in with her. "I'm lonely without Cassim," she said.

"We still have to keep our heads down," Ali Baba told them all. "We can't risk the thieves finding out we stole their treasure and that means not using it for a while."

The thieves, meanwhile, had discovered Cassim's body missing from the cave and were furious. Determined to discover who'd stolen him, they scoured the city, hot with vengeance. "Death to he who knows our password," they vowed.

Gamal told them to watch and wait.

After a couple of weeks, Cassim's widow decided Ali Baba was being over cautious. She liked to buy herself little treats, so she started to visit the market, spending some of the treasure Ali Baba had stolen from the cave.

One of the thieves recognized a necklace and reported back to Gamal, who laid his plans. He bought thirty-nine oil jars and piled them outside Ali Baba's new home. Inside each jar, a thief was curled up, hidden. Only one jar was filled with oil.

"When you hear me throw a pebble," Gamal whispered to his thieves, "that's your signal to attack." Then he knocked at the door.

"Please can you help me?" he asked. "I'm here to sell oil in the market tomorrow and I have nowhere to stay tonight..."

"You're welcome to stay with us," offered Ali Baba, who didn't recognize Gamal in his guise as an oil seller.

Cassim's widow was delighted to have a guest and ordered Morgiana to cook a grand meal for supper.

Halfway through, Morgiana ran out of oil. "I'm sure the oil seller won't mind if I use his," she thought, dipping her jug into a jar. She was astonished when a hollow voice inside the jar said, "Is this the signal, Gamal?"

"Is it?" echoed from every jar.

"Not yet," she replied in a deep voice, thinking quickly. Somehow the thieves had discovered them. That meant the oil merchant was probably the captain of the thieves himself. If she didn't act, the whole family would be attacked in their beds.

She filled a large saucepan with oil, boiled it on the fire until it spat, then splashed it into each jar. One by one, the thieves died.

Morgiana went back inside, to serve the meal and prepare for the most dangerous part of her plan.

After dinner, she dressed up, placing bangles on her arms, draping a scarf over her shoulders, and finally tying a dagger around her waist.

"Would you like me to dance for you?" she asked the family.

Ali Baba and his wife were puzzled but Cassim's widow thought it was an excellent idea. Morgiana began to spin, twirling gracefully, waving her arms above her head, getting faster... and faster...

At the height of her dance, she withdrew the dagger and stabbed Gamal to death.

Ali Baba was horrified. "What have you done?" he cried.

"Look more closely at him," Morgiana said.

Ali Baba did and gasped. "Gamal?"

"He was going to kill us all," explained Morgiana. "His thieves were hidden in the oil jars outside."

Ali Baba and his family were so grateful to Morgiana that they shared the thieves' treasure with her.

Free to spend it as they wished, they all lived happily ever after – and the treasure cave and magic password were remembered in their family for generations, long after the treasure had been spent.

Sir Gawain and the Loathly Lady

K ing Arthur and his knights rode out on many quests, rescuing damsels in distress and fighting for justice.

On one such adventure, King Arthur had to free a lady from an evil baron.

"You want her release?" screamed the baron. "Answer me this: what do women want most?"

"I'll find out," promised Arthur. He asked hundreds of women what was their heart's desire, but since each had a different reply – money, laughter, flattery, a gallant knight – he knew he was nowhere near the truth.

Then one day he met a hideous old hag, so ugly he turned away.

"Wait! I know of your search," she cackled. "What do women want most? Give me a reward and I'll tell you."

Arthur turned back to face her with a shudder and the hag hissed, "Women want their own way."

As she spoke, Arthur realized he had his answer. "Name your reward," he said.

"I want to marry a knight," she declared.

Arthur was horrified. He couldn't bind any of his friends to this grim fate.

"I'll do it," said Gawain, the kindest, most courteous of Arthur's knights, when he heard.

"I won't let you, she's too foul," Arthur insisted. But the hag was owed a reward and Gawain wouldn't change his mind.

At their wedding feast, no one rejoiced
and the other knights mocked him for his
bride's ugliness.

Alone in their chamber that night, even
Gawain's kindness
faltered, and he couldn't
look at his bride.

"Why?" she demanded.

"You're old... and so
ugly," he stuttered.

"Age means wisdom,"
she replied. "And ugliness means no one will
be jealous of me."

Impressed by her honesty and courage,
Gawain turned to face her. To his
astonishment, the hideous old hag had
vanished. In her place was a beautiful woman.

"I am Lady Ragnelle and was spellbound
by a terrible enchantment," she explained.
"Because you agreed to marry me, it is now

half-broken. I can be my true self by day and ugly at night, or ugly by day and my true self at night. Which shall it be? You choose."

Gawain knew how to answer. "No, dear wife, you should choose. After all, every woman wants to have her own way."

He had said the right thing. The spell was now completely broken. Gawain was overjoyed to have a wife as beautiful as she was wise, and as wise as she was courageous.

To Arthur's surprise, the very next day, the evil baron arrived at the castle to apologize. No longer evil, he turned out to be Lady Ragnelle's brother, who had also been enchanted. The shattering of her spell ended his and his wickedness was dissolved forever.

Thumbelina

There was once a woman who desperately wanted a child. She wanted one more than anything else in the world, so she went to a fairy for help.

The fairy couldn't bear to see anyone unhappy. "I'll give you a magic seed," she said. "Plant it and see what happens."

The woman was doubtful but she did as the fairy said. Instantly, the seed grew into a wonderful red-gold flower, so lovely that the woman kissed it. As she did, its petals opened to reveal a beautiful, tiny girl, no bigger than a thumb.

"I'll call you Thumbelina," smiled the woman, and made her a bed out of a walnut shell, with rose petal sheets.

Thumbelina lived happily with her mother, until one night when a hideous toad hopped through her bedroom window.

"Just the wife for my boy!" croaked the toad and stole Thumbelina as she slept.

Thumbelina woke up and screamed.

"Meet your husband," said the toad, gesturing to her large, lumpy son.

"But I don't want to marry a toad," said Thumbelina. "Please let me go home."

The toads ignored her pleas and imprisoned her on a lily pad in the middle of the river.

Thumbelina began to sob so loudly that all the fish in the river heard. As soon as the toads left to search for food, a shoal of fish swam over, nibbling through the stalk of the lily pad until it broke free.

Thumbelina sailed away, floating past villages, woods and wide green fields. A big brown beetle spotted her and dived down, grabbing her in his claws.

"Look what I found!" he boasted to his friends.

"Ugh, she's ugly," they said. "Take her away."

"Well, I don't want her if she's ugly," said the beetle and dropped Thumbelina in a field.

For tiny Thumbelina, the towering blades of grass were like a forest. She wove herself a bed out of a leaf, sucked honey from flowers and drank dewdrops. There she stayed happily, all summer long. Swallows sang and swooped around her, so she was never alone.

Then winter's icy breath sent the swallows away. Thumbelina grew cold and hungry.

"Would you like to share my home?" offered a kind field mouse, who had noticed Thumbelina shivering in the snow. The field mouse's home was snug, and a shelter from the bitter cold outside, but it was also gloomy. Thumbelina longed for the bright sun.

To cheer her up, the field mouse took Thumbelina to visit her friend the mole, a fat fellow in a black velvet suit. His house, full of rambling tunnels, was even gloomier, so dark that Thumbelina could barely see.

In one of the tunnels lay a swallow, deathly still. He had fallen through a hole in the roof.

"Died of cold," announced the mole. "Silly bird. Didn't fly away in time to escape winter."

Sadly, Thumbelina pressed her cheek against his feathery breast, remembering his sweet summer song. She thought she heard something... yes, a faint heart beat. "He's not dead, he's just frozen," she realized.

That night, she crept back to the swallow and covered him with a blanket of woven grass.

Slowly, the swallow opened his eyes.

"I'll keep you warm and take care of you," Thumbelina promised.

Every evening after that, Thumbelina brought him water, and seeds from the field mouse's store. By springtime, the swallow was well enough to leave.

"Come with me," he said, "and we can feel the sun on our backs."

"I'd love to," said Thumbelina, "but I can't leave the field mouse. She was so kind to me and I think she'd be unhappy if I left."

So the swallow flew off alone, leaving Thumbelina gazing sadly after him.

All through the summer, she longed to be living outside. The field mouse noticed how quiet and withdrawn Thumbelina had become.

"Don't fret!" she said. "I have some exciting news. Mole has decided to marry you."

Thumbelina gasped. "But I don't want to marry him."

The field mouse was shocked. "Why not? He's rich. He has a big house. What more do you want?"

"I don't want to spend the rest of my life underground," Thumbelina tried to explain. "I miss the sun and the sky."

"Don't be ungrateful," snapped the field mouse. "Your wedding day is tomorrow."

Thumbelina sneaked to the door of the field mouse's home, for one last look at the sky.

She heard a warbling above her, and there was the swallow.

"Winter is on its way," he said. "I'm leaving for warmer shores. Come with me?"

"Oh yes!" cried Thumbelina. She climbed onto his back and off they flew, over the sea to the warm countries where the skies were pure blue and wonderful flowers and fruit scented the air.

At last, they reached a palace surrounded by flowers, where the swallow had a nest.

He set her down by a large white flower. To Thumbelina's astonishment, out stepped a tiny man with a gold crown and butterfly wings. Every blossom had a similar fairy, but this one was the King.

"He's so handsome," she whispered to the swallow, while the fairy thought Thumbelina was the loveliest girl he'd ever seen.

"Will you be my bride?" he asked, and she answered, with a shy smile, "Oh yes."

At their wedding, the fairies gave her a pair of wings so she could join her husband, flying from flower to flower, and, high in his nest, the swallow sang her his sweetest song.

King Donkey Ears

Once upon a time, there lived a King with a terrible secret. His secret was so dreadful that only the servants who cut his hair knew it – and, each time one finished a haircut, the unfortunate soul was immediately thrown into prison.

One month, it was the turn of a young servant named Meg to cut the King's hair.

She carefully trimmed the back and the front. Then he removed his crown so she could reach the sides, and Meg nearly dropped her scissors in shock. The King had long, velvety donkey's ears on the top of his head.

"Oh!" Meg squeaked before she could stop herself. She continued to cut, as if nothing was wrong, but as soon as she had finished, the King announced her fate.

"You will now be taken to prison," he said. "No one must discover my secret."

"Please no," begged Meg. "My mother is sick at home. She can't live without me."

The King thought of his own mother and his heart softened. "You must promise NEVER to tell anyone," he said sternly.

"I promise," replied Meg.

"Then you may go," said the King. "But if you ever tell my secret..."

"I won't," Meg assured him.

She hurried home and her life continued as before, except that now the King's secret was burning inside her.

"I'll burst if I don't tell someone," she thought. Finally, she had an idea. "I promised I wouldn't tell *anyone*... so I'll tell a tree!"

Meg found the tallest tree in the densest forest. She put her lips to its trunk, whispered the King's secret and went home feeling much better.

A few weeks later, the tree was cut down and made into a harp. A few months after that, there was a grand concert at the palace.

The noblemen and women in the audience chattered excitedly, hushing as the harpist sat down at her new instrument.

She plucked intently at the strings, but the music that came out sounded very much like:

The King has donkey's ears!
The King has donkey's ears!

The King jumped to his feet. "Guards!" he bellowed. "Arrest that servant, Meg. She must have told my secret."

Meg cowered in the crowd, but then the King's best friend stepped forward. "It's not a secret, your Majesty," he said. "We all know."

"And you don't mind?" asked the King.

"Of course not!"

So the King freed all the servants... and he learned to love his ears.

The Little Red Hen

The little red hen was always very busy, scratching about in the farmyard for worms. But one day, instead of worms, she found a handful of wheat seeds.

"Cluck, cluck," she said delightedly, fluffing up her feathers. "Who will help me plant these seeds?"

"Meow," yawned the farm cat, who was lying on a haybale. "Not I."

"Eek-eek," squeaked a lazy rat, sprawled beside the cat. "Not I."

"Quack," squawked a duck, who was taking a break from splashing in the pond. "Not I."

"Well then, I'll plant them myself," said the little red hen. And she did.

The little red hen waited patiently until the wheat grew golden and tall. Then she clucked happily. "Who will help me harvest the wheat?"

"Not I," mewed the cat.

"Not I," quacked the duck.

"Not I," squeaked the rat.

"Well then, I'll harvest it myself," said the little red hen. And she did.

When all the wheat was picked and ready, the little red hen clucked again. "Who will help me mill the wheat into flour?"

"Not I," mewed the cat.

"Not I," quacked the duck.

"Not I," squeaked the rat.

"Well then, I'll mill it myself," said the little red hen. And she did.

Now she had a bag of fine, soft flour. "Who will help bake this flour into bread?" she asked.

"Not I," mewed the cat.

"Not I," quacked the duck.

"Not I," squeaked the rat.

"What a surprise," clucked the little red hen. "Well then, I'll bake it myself." And she did. The smell of fresh-baked bread drifted across the farmyard...

"Mmm," cried the cat, the duck and the rat, following their noses to see what it was. "That loaf you've made smells delicious! Can we help you eat it?"

"No!" laughed the little red hen. "I'm going to eat it *all by myself*." And she did.

The Magic Porridge Pot

Once upon a time, there was a little girl, who was so poor that she never had enough food to eat.

Every day she would go to the forest, searching for nuts and berries or fruits and honey to eat. Whatever she found, she shared with her family and friends.

One afternoon, she met an old woman.

"I want to help you," said the woman. "I've seen you looking for food and sharing what you find, so I'm going to give you this magic pot."

"What does it do?" asked the little girl.

"Whenever you are hungry, just say, "Cook pot, cook," and the pot will fill with warm and creamy porridge. When you've had enough, say, "Stop pot, stop!""

"Cook pot, cook!" said the little girl, and to her amazement, porridge filled the pot. It kept bubbling and bubbling until porridge was spilling down its sides.

"Stop pot, stop," ordered the old woman, and the pot stopped cooking.

The little girl grinned. "Now, let's eat!" she said, and the two sat down together to share a delicious meal of sweet, warm porridge.

"Remember the magic words," said the old woman, as she got up to go, "and you need never be hungry again."

The little girl ran all the way home, and showed the magic pot to her family. That night, they all had porridge for supper.

What they didn't know was that a greedy boy was watching through the window. He saw the pot start to cook, but he didn't see it stop.

When everyone had gone to bed, he crept into their cottage and stole the pot. Then he raced home with it under his arm, set it down in his bedroom and cried, "Cook pot, cook."

The pot began to cook. Porridge bubbled up to the top of the pot and dribbled down the sides.

"Stop!" said the little boy. But the pot didn't stop.

Porridge bubbled over his bedroom floor. It glooped its way down the stairs. It filled the hallway and burst through the front door.

"Stop! Stop!" shouted the boy, but still the pot didn't stop.

Porridge swept down the street like a lumpy, glutinous river. The boy waded through it crying, "Stop! Stop!" But the river of porridge ran on, past houses and over the hill.

"Help!" cried the boy. "I'm drowning in porridge."

The little girl looked out of her window, and saw what the little boy had done. "Stop pot, stop!" she cried. And, at last, the pot stopped.

The little boy was saved. But he had to eat his way through the river of porridge before he could get home again.

Fox and Stork

Fox adored playing tricks. He liked
playing tricks on Rabbit, and he liked
playing tricks on Weasel, but he *loved* playing
tricks on Stork. She was so kind and honest,
she never once suspected.

Whatever joke Fox came up with, Stork
fell for it every time. One afternoon, as Fox
was trotting through the forest, he had such a
brilliant idea, it made him laugh out loud. He
decided to invite Stork to his home for dinner.

That evening, Stork cleaned all her feathers, and flew to Fox's home, singing as she went. As Fox opened the door, Stork breathed in the delicious smell of Fox's rich onion soup.

"Mmm, that's the soup I like best!" said Stork, and she sat down at the table, eagerly eyeing up her dinner.

Fox grinned as he poured the soup into two wide, shallow bowls. Fox started lapping up his dinner, while Stork stared sadly at hers.

It was simply impossible for Stork to get at the soup with her long beak. However hard she tried, poor Stork couldn't eat a thing.

"Don't you like it?" asked Fox. Without giving her a chance to reply, he added, "Well, I suppose I'll have to eat yours, if you don't want it," and he poured all of Stork's soup into his own bowl, lapping that up too.

That night, Stork flew home, angry and hungry. The next morning, she was less hungry, but more angry. She was livid with Fox and his mean tricks. And then she had an idea of her own. She invited Fox for dinner.

That afternoon, Stork cooked her very best recipe. It used all the finest ingredients, and took her hours to make.

"Spicy pumpkin soup? That's the soup I like best!" declared Fox, as he arrived that evening. "It smells delicious."

"Thank you," Stork said, proudly.

As Fox sat at the dinner table, he licked his lips. He hadn't had anything to eat all day, and he was starving. Then his face fell.

Stork was pouring the soup into tall, slender jars. She placed the soup on the table, dipped her beak into her jar, and began to drink.

Fox dipped his snout into the top of the jar, but it didn't fit very far. He tried dipping his paw in and then shaking the jar. Nothing worked. However hard he tried, Fox couldn't get even the smallest taste of the soup inside. Finally, he gave up.

"You tricked me!" he shouted.

"That's true," said Stork, "but you tricked me first."

Fox slunk off to his den, a scowl on his face. He was hungry, miserable, and angry. No one had ever tricked him before, and he didn't like it at all.

"Always be kind to your friends," Stork called after him, "and they will be kind to you."

Brer Rabbit Down the Well

Usually, Brer Rabbit liked lolloping along, ears twitching, nose sniffing, eyes on the look out for mischief. But not today. Today, he was running so fast his breath came in short, sharp pants and his ears were flat against his back. He was being chased by his old enemy, Brer Fox.

"Wait till I get my paws on you!" shouted Brer Fox. "When I do, I'm going to eat you all up!"

Brer Rabbit ran faster. But he knew he couldn't keep it up for long. "I need... somewhere... to hide," he thought, his eyes darting left and right.

Up ahead, he saw a well. "Perfect," thought Brer Rabbit. "I'll hide in the bucket until Brer Fox has gone."

Brer Rabbit took a flying leap and landed neatly in the bucket. But then the bucket started to fall.

Weeeeeeeeeeeeeeeeeeeeeeeeeee it went, down and down, deeper and deeper into the deep, dark well.

"Aaaaaaargh!" screamed Brer Rabbit, his arms waving wildly, until the bucket landed at the bottom with an enormous SPLASH!

Brer Rabbit looked up. The walls of the well were steep and slippery. The sky looked very far away. "How am I ever going to get out?" he wondered.

Then the light was blotted out as Brer Fox peered in. "Ha, ha! Found you!" he mocked. "You can't hide from me..."

"I'm not hiding," Brer Rabbit replied, swishing his paw through the water. "I'm fishing. I'm having a mighty fine time down here."

"Fishing?" said Brer Fox.

"Oh yes!" said Brer Rabbit. "This well is the best fishing spot around. I've caught *one, two, three, four, five* fish, and I've only just started."

Brer Fox licked his lips. He just loved fish.

"You'd better come down here," taunted Brer Rabbit, "or there won't be any left."

Brer Fox began hauling up the bucket. He'd forgotten all about eating Brer Rabbit. He was dreaming of those fish.

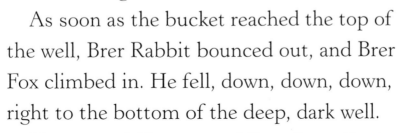

As soon as the bucket reached the top of the well, Brer Rabbit bounced out, and Brer Fox climbed in. He fell, down, down, down, right to the bottom of the deep, dark well.

"Aaaaaaargh!" screamed Brer Fox, clinging onto the sides of the bucket.

SPLOSH! SPLASH! He landed at the bottom. *Splish! Splish!* went his paws, swishing through the water.

"Brer Rabbit!" he growled, looking up. "Where are those fish?"

"Ha ha! Tricked you again, Brer Fox!" laughed Brer Rabbit. "There are no fish down there and now you're stuck."

And off went Brer Rabbit, lolloping along, *lippety-loppety, lippety-loppety*, ears twitching, nose sniffing, eyes on the look out for mischief.

As for Brer Fox, it took him a long, long time to climb out of that well.

Sinbad the Sailor

Sinbad the sailor was rich beyond his wildest imaginings. Travel and adventure had brought him all the wealth he could wish for... but Sinbad felt restless. He wanted to see the world, find out how other men lived and explore their cities and islands.

So he went to the market and bought silks and spices to trade. Then he joined a ship's crew and set out on the high seas. For days they sailed from island to island, trading their goods.

One day, they moored on an island covered in fruit trees. Sinbad lay down in the shade of a tree to doze.

When he awoke, his ship had already set
sail. "HELP!" he cried. "HELP!" But there
wasn't a soul to answer him.

Sinbad scrambled up a tree and saw that
on one side there was nothing but sea. On the
other, the empty island stretched out before
him – empty but for an
enormous, white egg.

Sinbad slid down the
tree and crept over to
look at the egg. As he
studied it, the sun was
blotted out by a bird as big as a cloud.

"A roc bird!" realized Sinbad, remembering
sailors' tales of a monstrous bird.

The roc settled down to sit on its egg, and
Sinbad planned his escape. He unwound the
turban on his head and tied it around the leg
of the bird. "When it flies away, it'll take me
with him!" he thought.

At the first light of dawn, the roc rose up on its enormous wings and flew so high Sinbad could no longer see the earth. He clung on tight, shutting his eyes until he felt the roc hit the ground with a bump.

Sinbad quickly untied his turban, just in time to see the bird snap up a terrifying serpent in its jaws, and fly off once more.

Sinbad groaned as he looked about him. He was even worse off than before. Now, he was trapped in a valley with steep sides. Dead sheep lay on the ground, and slithering towards him were snakes so big they could swallow an elephant.

The snakes were sliding over sparkling jewels that studded the dusty earth.

Sinbad grabbed
a few handfuls and
stuffed them in his pocket,
wondering how he would
ever escape.

More roc birds were circling
above him. Every now and then, one would
swoop down and grab a dead sheep in its
vicious claws.

"Aha!" thought Sinbad. Whipping off his
turban once again, he tied himself to a dead
sheep and waited. Sure enough, down came
a roc, grabbed the sheep... and they were off,
Sinbad trailing along behind.

As the roc bird flew over the ridge of
the valley, a group of men raced towards
it, waving their arms and forcing the roc to
drop the sheep. Sinbad undid himself, and
scrambled to one side, watching curiously as
the men searched the sheep's fleece.

"What are you doing?" he asked.

"We throw sheep into the valley, hoping to catch jewels in their fleece. Then we wait for the roc birds to bring them back up again."

"But how did *you* get here?" asked one of the men, looking at Sinbad. "Don't pretend you escaped from Snake Valley."

"It's a long story," said Sinbad. "But I do have some jewels..." He pulled them out of his pocket. "Will you take these for my passage home?"

The men nodded, listening in amazement to Sinbad as he shared his tale of adventure – and escape.

Mouse Deer and Tiger

Mouse Deer was small, but he was cunning. He had to be. He lived in a dangerous jungle, with tigers and cobras, crocodiles and leopards – and they *all* wanted to eat him.

One morning, as Mouse Deer drank from the river, he heard a low, rumbling *ROAR*...

"Tiger!" gasped Mouse Deer.

"Breakfast!" growled Tiger.

"I'm sorry, Tiger," said Mouse Deer, "but I can't be your breakfast." He looked around, thinking fast.

"I'm guarding the King's chocolate pudding."

"His chocolate pudding?" asked Tiger.

"Yes, there it is," said Mouse Deer, pointing to a pile of mud. "It's sweeter than nectar. More delicious than the freshest fruit. But no one is allowed to go near it."

"Can't I just have a tiny, tiny taste?" begged Tiger.

"Oh no," said Mouse Deer. "The King would be furious."

"*Please, please, pleeeease,*" purred Tiger.

"Very well then," said Mouse Deer. "But first I must flee from here, so I can pretend you chased me away." And Mouse Deer ran as fast as he could, deep into the heart of the jungle.

Tiger closed his eyes and took a great big mouthful.

"Urgh! Bleurgh!" he cried, choking on the mud. "You tricked me once, Mouse Deer. But next time, you'll be my lunch."

All morning, Tiger prowled through the jungle, looking for Mouse Deer. At last he found him, nibbling on some leaves.

"Tiger!" gasped Mouse Deer.

"Lunch!" growled Tiger.

"I'm sorry, Tiger," said Mouse Deer. "I can't be your lunch. I'm guarding the King's belt."

"The King's belt?" asked Tiger.

Mouse Deer pointed to a bright loop hanging from a branch overhead.

"It's the best belt in the world," said Mouse Deer. "But no one else is allowed to wear it."

"Can't I even try it on?" asked Tiger.

"Oh no," said Mouse Deer. "The King would be furious."

"*Please, please, pleeeease,*" purred Tiger.

"Very well then," said Mouse Deer. "But first I must flee from here, so I can pretend you chased me away." And Mouse Deer ran as fast as he could, heading deeper and deeper into the jungle.

Tiger coiled the belt around his waist, pulling it tight.

The belt began to hiss and coiled itself tighter.

"A snake!" cried Tiger, desperately trying to wriggle free.

"Wait till I get you, Mouse Deer. You tricked me once, you tricked me twice. But next time I'll eat you for my dinner!"

All afternoon, Tiger prowled through the jungle, looking for Mouse Deer. By evening, he found him, hiding in the darkest depths beside a tall tree.

"Tiger!" gasped Mouse Deer.

"Dinner!" growled Tiger.

"I'm sorry, Tiger," said Mouse Deer. "I can't be your dinner. I'm guarding the King's drum."

"The King's drum?" asked Tiger.

Mouse Deer pointed to a dark shape hanging from the tree.

"It makes the best sound in the jungle," said Mouse Deer. "No one else is allowed to touch it."

"Can't I tap it gently, very gently, just once?" begged Tiger.

"Oh no," said Mouse Deer. "The King would be furious."

"*Please, please, pleeeease,*" purred Tiger.

"Very well then," said Mouse Deer. "But first I must flee from here, so I can pretend you chased me away."

Mouse Deer ran, and this time he kept on running.

Tiger raised his paw and batted the drum. The drum began to buzz. It was a wasps' nest. Wasps poured out, surrounding Tiger in an angry swarm.

Then they began to sting.

"Argh! Eek! Ow!" cried Tiger and ran to the river to hide.

Only when they'd gone, did he dare creep out again. "I give up, Mouse Deer!" he roared into the night. "My mouth is full of mud, my stomach is covered in snake bites and my paws have been stung by wasps. I promise, I'll never try to eat you again."

Far away in the jungle, Mouse Deer heard Tiger's promise, and smiled.

The Sorcerer's Apprentice

There was once an old, wizened sorcerer, who had a young, naïve apprentice.

One day, the sorcerer announced he was going into town, leaving his apprentice alone in the workshop for the first time. The apprentice's eyes lit up, but the sorcerer met his gaze sternly.

"While I'm out," said the old man, "you can fill up the water tub – it's nearly empty – and then scrub the workshop floor."

"Yes, sir," replied the apprentice, obligingly, though a twinkle lingered in his eye.

Alone at last, the apprentice looked around the workshop. The water tub was massive, and the bucket to fill it tiny. It would take forever unless... unless... he followed his master's example and used some magic.

He spied a broomstick in the corner and the words of one of the sorcerer's spells tripped off his tongue:

Root and branch of old oak tree
Bring this broom to life for me.

At once, the broom began to twitch. It shook and it shuddered, then two skinny arms and two skinny legs sprouted from its handle.

The apprentice laughed and clapped his hands in delight.

"Now broom, take that bucket and get me some water," he ordered.

Without hesitating, the broom ran to the river, filled up the bucket, returned to the workshop and emptied the water into the tub. Quick as lightning it repeated its errand, again and again, neither slowing nor tiring.

In a flash, the water tub was nearly full.

"Great!" said the apprentice. "You can stop now."

The broom took no notice. Out it clattered once more, returning with another bucketful of water to tip into the precariously full tub.

"That's enough!" cried the apprentice. But the broom would not stop. It brought yet another bucketful of water and this time the tub overflowed.

"Just stop, will you?" pleaded the apprentice. "Oh, what's the magic spell to make it stop?"

He could not remember and without it, the broom was unstoppable. Now water was sloshing all over the workshop floor.

In desperation, the apprentice picked up one of the sorcerer's axes. Lifting it high above his head, he waited for the broom to come near, then swung it down hard.

CRACK.

The broom split clean in two.

Alas, the apprentice's problem was not solved; it was doubled. The two halves of the broom both sprouted new limbs and continued the job of getting, carrying and emptying the water, only now there was twice the amount coming in.

Waves washed across the workshop floor, and soon the water was up to the apprentice's knees... then his waist... then his chest...

"MASTER!" he yelled in panic. "HELP!"

Suddenly, there was the sorcerer, taking in the scene and calmly raising his wand.

Back now broom, return
To how you were before,
Until I, the real master,
Call for you once more.

The Nutcracker

It was Christmas Eve. Clara was far too excited to sleep. They'd had a party, and Clara's godfather had put her present under the tree. He always gave her the most interesting presents.

Quietly, she slipped out of bed and crept downstairs... "One little peep won't hurt," she thought, tearing a corner of the paper. There was a nutcracker doll, dressed as a soldier.

Clara suddenly felt so extraordinarily tired that she curled up and fell asleep, right there, under the tree. When she woke, the tree was huge. "Have I shrunk?" she wondered.

She jumped to her feet in a panic, but a friendly voice said, "Hello. I'll take care of you. I'm the Nutcracker Prince."

Clara gasped. Her doll had come alive!

"Don't be alarmed but the mice are plotting to capture you," the prince went on. He blew a whistle and a line of toy soldiers marched up, just as a band of evil mice charged from the shadows, led by the Mouse King.

"Fire!" ordered the prince and the soldiers shot lumps of cheese from toy cannons. Several mice scampered after the cheese, but victory was not yet won.

"Is that the best you can do?" jeered the Mouse King. "Hand over the girl."

"Never!" said the prince.

A fierce battle followed. In desperation, Clara flung her slipper at the Mouse King's head. He fell down, knocked out cold, and the prince raced to Clara's side.

"Brilliant work!" he laughed. "Come on, let's celebrate."

They jumped into a golden sleigh drawn by reindeer, and flew off into the snowy night.

Stars spun past as they soared through the sky, coming down to land by the Ice Queen's shimmering, frosty palace.

"Welcome," said the Queen, taking them to a ballroom where ballerinas in white and silver dresses danced more beautifully than Clara had ever seen.

Before long, the prince was whirling her away again. "To the Land of Sweets!" he cried.

Clara couldn't stop smiling at the chocolate mountains speckled with sugared roses, and trees blossoming with marshmallows. A fairy dressed from head to toe in pink, danced out of a gingerbread castle and kissed them both.

"I'm the Sugarplum Fairy. Please join our party."

Entranced, Clara watched an Arab princess dancing to soft music; a Spanish couple twirling to snapping castanets, and Chinese dancers leaping on nimble feet.

Finally, she saw ballerinas, each dressed as a flower, spinning around in a glorious, graceful dance.

"Time for us to go," said the prince.

Reluctantly, Clara jumped back in the sleigh, and fell asleep on the prince's shoulder.

When she woke, she found herself in her own home, lying under the Christmas tree her own size, and holding her godfather's present – the nutcracker doll. The prince had disappeared.

"It was all a dream," she murmured. "The most wonderful dream anyone could ever have. I'll never forget. Never, never, ever."

Then... was it her imagination, or did her doll give her a friendly wink?

The White Bear King

Far away to the north, where the land is covered in snow, a poor family lived in a small stone cottage. They sat huddled around a fire to keep out the cold, listening to the wild, whistling wind. Suddenly, there was a knock at the door.

"Who could be out on a night like this?" asked the father, opening the door.

A large, white bear stood before him, raised up on its strong hind legs. As the father stared in shock, the bear spoke.

"I mean you no harm," he said. "I have come to offer

for your youngest daughter. I know you are poor and I will give you great riches in return. I promise to keep her safe."

"No," said the father, "I cannot let her go. She is more precious to me than riches."

But his youngest daughter stepped forward. "Let me go with him," she begged. "Our clothes are tattered rags. We have no food. Like this, we cannot survive the winter."

Before her parents could stop her, she walked out into the night. The bear dropped down on all fours. She swung herself onto the bear's back. "Take hold of my fur," he said, and they rode away beneath the stars.

They crossed moors and rivers and wove their way through thick forests, until at last they came to a craggy mountain.

At the bottom was a door, hidden between the rocks. The bear knocked three times and it opened, revealing a secret, golden castle.

"Here is a silver bell," said the bear. "Ring it whenever you need anything."

The girl rang the bell and found herself in a stately bedroom hung with beautiful silks. Too tired to think any more, the girl lay down and slept.

As the months passed, she wanted for nothing. Food and clothes were brought to her and by day she could wander over the castle. But loneliness gnawed at her like hunger for she rarely saw the bear. When she did, he would rest his soft head on her lap and let her stroke him, his eyes shining with secrets.

One night, she saw a man in the shadows, dragging a bearskin. "Is it the bear changed into a man?" she wondered. When she asked, the bear replied, "Don't ask me such questions. Please try to be happy as you are."

"I must find out," decided the girl. That night, she took a candle and searched for the man.

She found him sleeping in one of the high turrets of the castle. Bending over, she gasped to see his handsome face in the flickering candlelight. But a drop of hot wax landed on his shoulder, and woke him.

"What have you done?" he cried. "I am a prince bewitched by the Troll Queen – made bear by day, man by night."

He sighed, and went on. "The spell would only be broken if I could find a girl who would love me for a year, without seeing my human face. Now I must go to the Troll Queen and marry her, in the castle that lies east of the sun and west of the moon."

As he spoke, the castle crumbled around them. The girl found herself standing on rocky ground, and the prince had vanished.

"I will go after him," she vowed. "I will head north for that is where the trolls live."

It was a long, weary way. "Help me!" she called to the East Wind. "I need to find the castle that lies east of the sun and west of the moon."

"I have never blown that far," the East Wind replied. "I will take you to my brother, the West Wind, for he is much stronger than I."

But when they arrived in the land where the West Wind lived, he could not help them. "I have never blown that far," he said. "I will take you to my brother, the South Wind."

Balancing the girl on his head, he flew to the land where the South Wind lived.

"Only the North Wind knows the way to the castle," said the South Wind. "For he is the oldest and the strongest of us all."

The North Wind reached out for the girl with his icy breath and carried her on his back. He blew for many days, raging over oceans and stormy seas.

At long last, they reached the castle. "I must rest here," said the North Wind, in ragged, panting breaths. "Good luck, my child."

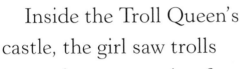

Inside the Troll Queen's castle, the girl saw trolls everywhere, preparing for the wedding.

"If he is not yet married, I still have time," the girl murmured. She walked in the shadows, searching for the prince, until at length she found him, fast asleep in the Troll Queen's tallest tower.

The girl shook him. She called to him, but nothing would wake him. In desperation, she took a burning candle from the wall and held it over him, until a drop of hot wax fell onto his shoulder. The prince woke, as if a spell had broken.

"You found me," he said, a smile on his face. "You've found me in time."

Together they ran out of the castle, racing past the Troll Queen's guards. When they reached the icy shore, they saw a boat, bobbing on the water and leaped aboard. The North Wind blew them home.

Finally stepping off the boat, the girl turned to the North Wind and asked, "Why did you and your brother winds help me?"

"Your story was foretold to us," the North Wind replied. "For you are the girl who went to the ends of the Earth for love."

The Golden Goose

Once, a woodcutter and his wife had three sons. The youngest was named Dumbling, and everyone thought him dim-witted, even his own family.

One morning, the woodcutter didn't feel well, so his eldest son went to cut the wood.

"Take this for your lunch," said his mother, packing up a freshly-baked pie.

The son chopped and chopped until midday, when a little old man appeared.

"Any food for me?" he asked.

"No. I'll have none left," said the boy, stuffing himself.

When he began chopping again, he cut his arm and had to stop.

So the next day, the second son went to chop wood. The old man popped up again and asked for a little food.

"What I give you, I won't have for myself. Go away!" said this son, munching greedily. Shortly after that, he nicked his leg chopping wood and had to limp home.

"I'll go," said Dumbling, the next morning.

"You? Ha! Ha!" laughed his family, but there was no one else to send.

Off Dumbling went, with a stingy picnic of bread and water. When the old man appeared and asked for food, Dumbling said, "Of course. We'll share everything I have."

"Thank you," said the old man, adding before he disappeared, "Your reward is in the next tree you cut."

Dumbling carried on chopping and there, nestling in a tree trunk, was a golden goose.

Dumbling put it to one side, and kept on chopping. At dusk, he picked it up and decided to spend the night at a nearby inn.

The innkeeper's eldest daughter saw the goose, with its gleaming golden feathers, and told her two sisters about it.

In the early light of dawn, they crept to Dumbling's room. The eldest sister went to pluck a feather, but the second she touched the goose, she stuck to it. Her alarmed sisters tried to pull her free and they stuck to her.

Dumbling, woken by their shouts, tried to wrench his goose away, but he couldn't shake off the girls. He ran outside in a panic, followed by three screaming sisters, all still attached to each other.

"Where do you think you're going?" yelled their mother, grabbing the youngest girl. Instantly she was stuck too.

"STOP!" shrieked the innkeeper, seizing his wife. Now there was a line of people running down the street, Dumbling with his golden goose, the three girls, the innkeeper's wife and the innkeeper himself, all stuck fast. They ran on and reached a castle.

Now, in this castle lived the most serious princess in the world. She had never smiled or laughed in her life. Her father, the King, was in such despair, he'd even announced a new law: "Whoever makes my daughter laugh shall have her hand in marriage and inherit the kingdom."

The princess happened to look out of the window and saw Dumbling, the golden goose and the line of people, one behind the other, shouting, running and stumbling along the road. She smirked... then she smiled... and then she laughed and laughed.

"Marry her!" the King said to Dumbling.

"I certainly will," agreed Dumbling, struck by her beauty.

As he spoke, the old man appeared and made everyone come unstuck. The wedding took place immediately.

When the King died, Dumbling took over the kingdom, and turned out to be a very wise ruler indeed.

The Snow Queen

O nce, there was a
wicked sprite.
He made a mirror, a
magical mirror, that
made everything
good and beautiful
look horrible and mean.

He flew around with it, this way and
that, but in his excitement he dropped it.

The mirror fell to earth, where it was
dashed into a hundred million pieces,
each hardly bigger than a grain of sand. When
the pieces got into people's eyes, there they
stayed, and then those people saw the world
in a terrible, twisted way.

Sometimes a piece would go into someone's
heart, and the heart became like a lump of ice.

The sprite laughed to see what had happened, and still the splinters flew around in the air... and now you shall hear what happened next.

In a crowded town of higgledy-piggledy houses, lived two children, Kay and Gerda, who loved each other as if they were brother and sister. In summer, they played together on the rooftops, or chatted across window-boxes of roses. In winter, they huddled together in Gerda's house, while her grandmother told them stories of the Snow Queen.

"She flies through the streets at night," said Grandmother, "and freezes all she looks at."

"Just let her come here," said Kay. "I'd put her on the stove to melt."

One evening, when Kay
was at home, he looked
out of his window and
saw a flake of snow,
growing larger and
larger, until at last
it became a woman.
She was beautiful but
stern, and seemed to
be made of shimmering,
sparkling ice. She beckoned to Kay,
but he was frightened and turned away.

At last, winter turned to spring, and then
summer, and the roses bloomed. Kay and
Gerda admired the roses, and it was then that
Kay cried, "Oh! I feel such a sharp pain in my
heart... and there's something in my eye."

Splinters of the sprite's mirror had pierced
his eye and lodged in his heart.

"I think it's out now," said Kay.

But it was not. "Look at that rose," he went on. "It's so ugly. Ha! You're ugly too, Gerda." Then he kicked the roses with his foot and ran away.

All that summer he teased Gerda and mocked her. When winter came again, he didn't want to sit by the fireside, listening to stories. Instead he took his sled and ran into the town square.

Spying a huge sleigh whizzing over the ice, Kay tied his little sled to it. Off they raced beyond the town, into the swirling snow.

When the sleigh stopped and the driver stepped out, Kay saw it was the Snow Queen herself. She was tall and slender, and wore a cloak and hat of dazzlingly white snow.

The Snow Queen drew Kay into her arms and kissed him. Her kiss was colder than ice. She kissed Kay once more and he forgot all about Gerda, her grandmother and his home.

In the town, nobody knew where Kay had gone. Gerda missed him dreadfully, despite his teasing, and when winter was over, she put on her red shoes and went down to the river.

"Have you seen Kay?" she asked the river. "If I give you my shoes, will you take me to him?" The river seemed to nod as it rippled, so she threw in her shoes, but they floated back to her.

"Perhaps I didn't throw them far enough," thought Gerda and climbed into a little boat by the bank.

She didn't realize it wasn't fastened, and it floated away down the river. Gerda was afraid, but there was no turning back.

As dusk fell, the river brought Gerda to a thatched cottage with red and blue windows. An old woman was in the garden tending her roses. She reached out for Gerda's boat with a crooked stick.

"Poor little child," she said. "Come and tell me who you are and how you came here."

Gerda told her all. The old woman shook her head, saying she hadn't seen Kay, and offered Gerda ripe, juicy cherries. Then she took out a golden comb, and combed Gerda's hair, combing away her memories as well.

She wasn't a wicked woman, she just longed for a little girl of her own.

She made the rose bushes sink into the ground, in case they reminded Gerda of home. And so the summer days began to pass...

...until, one day, Gerda saw a rose, painted on the old woman's sun hat.

In a rush, her memories came flooding back. "Oh! How long have I stayed!" cried Gerda. And she burst into tears, which fell to the ground, bringing the buried roses back to life.

Gerda knelt down beside them. "Do you think Kay is dead?" she asked the roses.

The roses shook their heads. "He is not dead. We have been in the earth where all the dead are, but Kay was not there."

"Then I must keep looking," cried Gerda.

She ran out of the garden, back into the
wild world, now shedding its leaves with the
end of summer. Gerda's feet were weary and
the search seemed so long, and so hard, that
she curled up on the ground and began to cry.

"Why are you sad, little girl?" called a raven
from his perch.

Gerda told him her tale and he nodded with
excitement. "I think I have seen Kay! I think
he has forgotten you for a princess."

"Oh please take me to him," begged Gerda.

"Follow me," called the raven.

The raven led Gerda to a palace. Her heart beat with anxiety and longing.

They were crossing an echoing hall, when Gerda stopped. "I think there is somebody just behind us," she said, and something rushed past, like a shadow on the wall.

"They are dreams," said the raven, "come to take royal thoughts for midnight rides."

At last, they reached the royal bedchamber. The ceiling was like a palm tree, with leaves of glass, and from it hung two beds that looked like flowers. In the first lay the princess, fast asleep, and in the second...

"Oh! That's Kay!" thought Gerda.

She called his name and he woke, turned his head and... it was not Kay.

Gerda sobbed, waking up the princess too.

"What is the matter?" she asked.

Gerda told her story, and the prince offered her his bed for the night. The next morning, she was given a carriage of pure gold to continue her journey.

Near dusk, the carriage entered a dark forest, shining like a sunbeam. It caught the eyes of some robbers, who rushed at it, crying, "'Tis gold! 'Tis gold!"

As they pulled Gerda out, a little robber girl called for them to stop. "I will ride with her,"

 she said, taking the carriage to the robbers' castle, high upon a craggy rock.

That night, Gerda could not sleep. Some wood pigeons fluttered down, softly calling to her. "Coo, coo! We have seen Kay. He is with the Snow Queen, carried away in her sleigh. She was headed for Lapland."

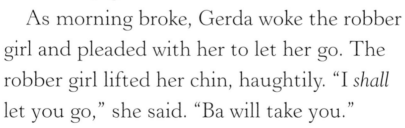

"How do I get to Lapland?" she asked.

"Ask Ba, the robber girl's reindeer," said the wood pigeons.

As morning broke, Gerda woke the robber girl and pleaded with her to let her go. The robber girl lifted her chin, haughtily. "I *shall* let you go," she said. "Ba will take you."

Gerda climbed onto his back. "Farewell!" she called, and the reindeer sped on, over bush and bramble, through great woods and over moor and heath, as fast as he could go. On and on they flew, to the icy, frozen north.

Ba set her down outside the Snow Queen's palace. "I can't take you any further," he said. "But you are good and sweet and innocent. You need no more help from me."

Gerda ran on as fast as she could.

Snowflakes whirled around her – enormous, living snow flakes, for these were the Snow Queen's guards.

They made terrifying shapes, hissing serpents, snarling bears and spiky porcupines.

Gerda cried out in fear, but she didn't run away. Her breath came out like mist from her mouth and formed angels that fought the guards.

Hurrying on, Gerda came to the walls of the palace, which were made of driving snow, and battled her way through entrance gates of biting winds.

Inside, she wandered through endless, empty halls of snow, lit by the Northern Lights. And, in the very middle of the palace, on a frozen lake, Gerda at last found Kay. He sat still... so still he seemed to be frozen stiff.

"Kay!" she called, running up to him. She hugged him, her hot tears dripping onto Kay's chest. They reached right through to his heart, thawing the lump of ice.

She talked to him of home, and her words and his melting heart brought tears to Kay's eyes too, washing away the splinter there.

"Gerda!" he cried.

"Is it really you?"

Gerda held him fast and wept for joy.

"How cold it is in here," said Kay. "How empty and cold."

Gerda kissed his eyes and they shone like her own.

"We must hurry," said Kay. "We must leave before the Snow Queen returns."

They took each other by the hand and tore out of the castle, laughing with relief.

Ba was waiting to carry them home. At long last, they arrived at Gerda's house, where her grandmother was overjoyed to see them.

"This is truly a fairytale ending!" cried the grandmother and the roses in the window-box nodded their heads, as if to agree.

The End

Edited by Lesley Sims Designed by Sam Chandler
Additional designs by Caroline Day, Holly Lamont, Russell Punter,
Alice Reese and Caroline Spatz
Cover design and illustration by Nancy Leschnikoff
Digital imaging by Nick Wakeford and Mike Olley

First published in 2012 by Usborne Publishing Ltd., 83-85 Saffron Hill, London EC1N 8RT, England.
www.usborne.com Copyright © 2012 Usborne Publishing Limited. The name Usborne and the devices ♀⬚ are
Trade Marks of Usborne Publishing Ltd. All rights reserved. No part of this publication may be reproduced, stored
in a retrieval system, or transmitted in any form or by any means, electronic, mechanical, photocopying, recording
or otherwise, without the prior permission of the publisher. First published in America in 2012. UE.